CYNTHIA HICKEY

GUIDING WITH LOVE

Finding Love the Harvey Girl Way
Book 2

Cynthia Hickey

Copyright © **2015**
Written by: Cynthia Hickey
Published by: Winged Publications
Cover Design: Cynthia Hickey

This book is a work of fiction. Names, characters, places, and incidents are the product of the author's imagination and are used fictitiously. Any resemblance to actual events, locales, or persons, living or dead, is coincidental.

No part of this book may be copied or distributed without the author's consent.
All rights reserved.

ISBN-13: 979-8-8690-9038-6

DEDICATION

As always, to my husband, Tom, and to God. Both who never give up on me.

I will praise you because I am fearfully and
wonderfully made;
Your works are wonderful,
I know that full well.

Psalm 139:14

1

Williams, Arizona, April 1905

Annie Rollins adjusted her new skirt and smiled at her reflection. How liberating! After making sure her hair stayed secure in its new style, backcombed so it stood inches higher than normal, she felt like a modern woman, even stuck in the backwoods of northern Arizona. With one final glance and pat at her pompadour, Annie sashayed from the room.

"What are you wearing?" Her mother's reaction did not disappoint.

"It's a split skirt, Mother." Annie twirled. "Do you like it? It offers so much freedom of movement."

Her mother planted her fists on her thin hips. "I do not, and what did you do to your hair? It's sky-high. Heaven have mercy."

"It's called a transformation. It's the newest style." Annie brushed past her and glided down the stairs. She might as well get the day started, and one of her jobs was to register guests at the B and B's front desk.

Her mother's heels tapped behind her. "Why do you feel the need to be highfalutin way out here?"

"There's nothing wrong with being modern. We're in the twentieth century." *Lord, give me strength.* Mother complained more often than not, ever since Papa's death two years ago. It was time to start living again.

"You look ridiculous and out of place in Williams." Mother unlocked the cabinet where she kept the registry book. She lifted the leather volume and plopped it on the counter. "People will laugh."

"Let them." Annie let the cover fall open and ran her finger down the page. "Only two guests registered?"

"Hopefully, there will be more. These two reservations came in by telegram."

Annie leaned her elbows on the counter. "I have an idea."

Her mother rolled her eyes. "Not another one. You and your harebrained schemes."

"We need to entice people to stay here. Offer them extra services." Annie raised her eyebrows, choosing to ignore her mother's attitude. "Have you thought any about my suggestion of offering guided tours of the canyon? I mentioned the idea to you weeks ago. I could be the guide. You know I would love it."

"Absolutely not." Mother shook her head. "That is definitely not a ladylike occupation."

"Sometimes I don't want to act like a lady." Annie lifted her chin. "Ladies don't have a lot of fun."

Mother's hand fluttered to her chest. "What am I going to do with you?"

"Let me be who I am." Annie sighed. Maybe a

change of subject was in order. "The new restaurant opens today. Should we eat dinner there?"

"What's wrong with my food?"

"Nothing. It was only a suggestion." It seemed Annie couldn't get anything right in her mother's eyes. Maybe she shouldn't try. Mother hadn't been happy when they'd moved from Boston to northern Arizona, but since Papa's death she seemed to want everyone around her to feel unhappy too.

"No more suggestions." Mother took a deep breath. "Starting tomorrow, I will be running the boardinghouse alone."

Annie fixed a stare on her. "What do you mean?" Please say she wasn't being sent to a school for ladies. That would be a fate worse than death.

Mother pulled a sheet of paper from her apron pocket. "Tomorrow morning you will report to the El Tovar. I got you a job as a Harvey Girl."

"What? Why? What about helping you?" It wasn't as bad as boarding school, but almost. "What about the women's ministry at church?" What about interviewing for the job herself?

"You have Sundays off." Mother slapped the application on the counter. "They've also agreed to allow you to sleep here rather than in the girls' dormitory. I promised them you were a comely girl with high moral standards and that I was more than sufficient as a chaperone during your off hours."

No doubt there. "So you aren't even going to consider my idea of guided tours?" Annie's shoulders slumped. Why couldn't Mother commend her, just once, for having a creative mind?

"I didn't say I wouldn't consider it, but that is a

man's job." Mother wiped her hands on her apron. "Time for work." She turned and unlocked the front door. Business as usual.

Annie blinked against the tears stinging her eyes. Nineteen years old, and she still wasn't in control of her own life. Didn't God give His children the desires of their hearts? Hers was to work outside in His creation, not in a stuffy restaurant.

"I need some air." Annie bolted from behind the counter and dashed outside.

"Annette Rollins." Her mother's screech followed. "Ladies do not run!"

Annie pinched the bridge of her nose between her forefinger and thumb, and then lifted her gaze to the new restaurant. Her prison.

The two-story El Tovar Hotel, built from local limestone and pine, overshadowed the dwellings around it. It was only a matter of time before the Rollins Boardinghouse would be out of business in favor of something grander. That was the main reason Annie presented new ideas to her mother for drawing in business. She didn't want to see her mother thrust out of her livelihood. If only she would listen!

Annie turned and surveyed the rim of the Grand Canyon, barely visible behind the hotel. Her heart yearned to explore the canyon floor, but even she knew it wasn't wise to go alone. Taking a group with her seemed the most sensible way. She headed toward her favorite view.

One of God's wonders for sure, and the real draw to the town of Williams, regardless of what the railroad people said. It might be the trains that brought the crowds, but it was the canyon that made them return.

Annie stopped at the edge and flung her arms wide, taking in the azure sky and the pinks and mauves of the plunging canyon walls. The Colorado River wound like a ribbon along the floor far below. A bald eagle soared under her, bobbing and dancing on the wind's current. What would that feel like—the freedom to soar?

Although the boardinghouse demanded plenty of hard work, it was home. It was all Annie knew. Now, she was being thrust into strange surroundings. Though her mother hadn't spelled it out, Annie was sure this new job was supposed to teach her feminine ways. She'd seen the waitresses flitting around town and going in and out of the hotel in their black-and-white uniforms. They looked fetching, but such a life wasn't for Annie.

She wanted so much more. Letting the tears fall, she lifted her desire to heaven. God would take care of the details. If she could step back and let Him.

*

Dallas Baker slung his saddlebags from the back of his horse to his shoulder, handed the reins to an older man waiting to take them, and then climbed the stairs to Rollins Boardinghouse. The newspaper advertisement in Dallas, Texas, his hometown and namesake, had come as the answer to a prayer. He didn't hate the rancher's way of life, but wanted something different. Somewhere he didn't have to work under his two older brothers. Love them he did, but not as bosses.

Stamping the mud from his boots, he pushed open the front door and stepped inside. The entryway made a person feel at home, with its hand-braided rugs and polished counter. His footsteps thudded on a scarred but polished wood floor, announcing his arrival. Why some folks preferred fancy hotels over a place that felt like home was beyond him.

An attractive middle-aged woman entered from a room on his right. "Welcome. I am the owner, Mrs. Rollins. Do you have a reservation?"

"No. I'm Dallas Baker, ma'am, your trail guide." He grinned.

"Our what?" A high-pitched voice of protest sounded behind him.

Dallas turned to see the prettiest gal he'd seen in a long time. Blond hair high on her head, flashing green eyes, and wearing a brown…what? "I'm the new canyon guide for the Rollins Boardinghouse," he told her.

Miss Attitude marched past him and stood in front of the proprietor. "Mother, how could you? This is my dream." She pounded one fist on her chest. "Mine. And you went behind my back—"

"I'll just step into the parlor." Neither woman glanced his way as he ducked out of sight. Nothing made Dallas skedaddle faster than an upset woman, and he'd managed to step between two of them. And what was the younger one wearing? It looked like a skirt, but was split like pants and was wide. Real wide. His mother would never be caught dead in that getup, and she was active on the ranch.

He set his bags on the floor and tried not to listen to the argument in the next room, wanting to be anywhere but where he was at the moment. Maybe he should go back outside. But that would take him past them again. He sighed and lowered himself onto a flowered sofa.

"You took my idea and went behind my back and hired a man." The younger woman's voice rose. "Have you absolutely no confidence in my abilities?"

"Annette, I will not be spoken to in this way. It's a fine idea, but not one suited for a woman. You need to learn your place in the world."

Dallas nodded. A true sentiment, indeed.

"And my place is dressed as a fancy crow at El Tovar?"

"If that's what it takes to teach you how to be a lady, then yes." Mrs. Rollins's words were clipped and cold.

Dallas had run across a few Harvey Girls on his travels. The term *crow* did not suit the women at all. They were refined and mannerly, making a man's travels easier with their femininity and smiles. But then he'd been told by more than a few women that he possessed backward ideas about a woman's role in today's modern world.

"Mr. Baker, you may come in now," Mrs. Rollins called. "My daughter will behave herself and, hopefully, offer no more embarrassment. We have an older gentleman who helps with the livery and the horses, so I'm sure you'll settle in quickly."

Heart in his throat, Dallas hefted his bags and rejoined the women. The younger one stood to the side, arms crossed. When she caught sight of him, she visibly struggled to maintain control of her emotions. High spots of color dotted her pale cheeks.

"I will show you to your room." Chin tilted high, Annette headed up the stairs.

Dallas hurried after her. "I'm sorry if I stepped on your toes. I'm here because of an advertisement. I've actually been in contact with your mother for a few weeks."

"Don't worry yourself, Mr. Baker. Our family

concerns are not yours." She pulled a key from a hidden pocket in her skirt and inserted it into a door on the second floor. "I hope the accommodations are to your liking."

He peered inside, more than pleased with the large bed covered with a colorful quilt. A small table held a gas lamp. A dresser stood against one wall and an upholstered chair against another. "More than sufficient, thank you."

"Let us know if you need anything else." Without meeting his gaze, she handed him the key and stepped back. "I'm Annie. Just give me a holler."

The nickname definitely suited the spitfire better than the more formal sounding name. "Thank you. I'll be fine."

With a nod, Annie stomped down the stairs. Moments later, Dallas heard the front door slam. "Whew. That one is something else." He tossed his bags on the bed and grinned. "But she sure is pretty."

Life promised to be very interesting.

*

Annie kept running until she reached her favorite spot to be alone, a fallen log that overlooked the canyon. She came here so often the rough bark was as familiar as Mother's rocking chair. How Annie missed her papa. She wiped away escaping tears. She and Papa had come to this exact spot every evening after supper, taking in God's glory, and letting the cares of the day blow away on the breeze.

She sighed and sat. Clouds drifted past her, lower than her feet. Annie almost felt as if she could walk on them to reach the other side of the great expanse. She caught glimpses of the Colorado River meandering at the bottom like a silver ribbon. She so wanted to go down there. Someday she would. Even if she had to go alone.

No handsome hired trail guide would take that pleasure away from her. This was her place, not a stranger's.

2

The next morning, Annie climbed the stairs to the impressive El Tovar Hotel. The Queen of the Canyon, she was called. It wasn't hard to agree, not with the sprawling split levels, one towering as high as four stories.

With shaking hands, Annie pushed the door open. What had her mother been thinking? Annie a waitress! She shook her head and asked God for help. There was no way she could serve food without spilling it unless Divine hands helped.

She stepped into the foyer and surveyed the open space, waiting for someone to greet her. A Hopi Indian bellhop shot her a curious glance. Annie smiled and continued studying the grandeur around her. Electric lights blazed from strategic places. One more strike against the Rollins Boardinghouse, which still used gas lanterns. Annie sighed. How would her mother make ends meet with such a modern hotel close by?

"You must be Annette. You look exactly as your mother described." A plump woman in the Harvey Girl uniform bustled forward. Her gaze flicked toward Annie's split skirt, then back to her face. To the woman's credit, she didn't say a word in regard to Annie's attire. "I'm the head waitress, Miss Cartwright, and I'm pleased to meet you. I've met your mother, you poor thing. I will set you to work at the lunch counter once you're trained."

Annie raised her eyebrows. Certainly Mother was a handful, but why would a complete stranger talk about her so negatively? "Yes, I'm Annie Rollins."

"Let's get you fitted for your uniform. Since we opened, the place has moved as fast as the trains that bring our guests. Mr. Harvey, bless his soul, set strict guidelines in place before his death. Now, his company still carries those same values." Miss Cartwright swept aside her flowing skirts and stepped through a door. Annie followed, trying not to slow down and gawk at the wonders of the place.

"Our seamstress, Mrs. Oakley, is truly gifted in the art of the needle." The head waitress pushed through another door, this one leading to the kitchen.

Annie's mouth opened in surprise. How her mother would love the massive stove and walk-in pantry. They could feed all of Williams from here. Maybe Annie could come up with a way to help the boardinghouse so that her mother would not need to work hard to compete where she was bound to lose.

"Here we are." Miss Cartwright beamed, opening a door off a hallway leading from the kitchen. "Once you have your uniform, come to the dining room, and we'll get you situated right away."

Annie forced a smile. My, how she did rattle on, but one couldn't help but feel welcome in the friendly woman's presence.

"I run a tight ship here, but I try to do so with a firm and loving hand. No complaints so far." Miss Cartwright smiled again. "Mrs. Oakley, here is our new girl, Annie Rollins."

A woman as round as she was tall sat in a rocking chair in front of a line of black dresses. "Why, you're a tall, willowy thing, aren't you? And as lovely as the sunset over this grand canyon of ours. Oh, a split skirt. You must be quite the adventurous sort."

"I like to think so." Annie stood in front of her.

"I'll leave you two to get busy." Miss Cartwright backed out of the room.

The seamstress heaved her bulk from her chair and reached for a box above her head. "The bow will look grand in that pouf of yours."

"Let me help you." Annie reached up and easily grasped the box.

"Thank you, child. Now take a bow, and in the basket there are aprons. On the shelf over there are shoes." Mrs. Oakley ran her hand along the gowns, finally choosing one. "I think this will fit. Might have to let the hem down a bit, but you'll be a vision of loveliness. Pretty as a swan."

"Or a stork," Annie muttered.

Mrs. Oakley chuckled. "You have a fine sense of humor, too. You'll make some man a good wife."

"I'm not looking to get married. At least not for a long while. I have dreams of leading groups of people into the canyon."

"Oh, well." Mrs. Oakley's eyes widened. "Ever done that before?"

"No, but I aim to learn." She almost revealed how much her mother detested her dreams, but years of hearing how one mustn't air one's dirty laundry echoed.

"I reckon you're a gal who might just do that." Mrs. Oakley handed her the dress. "Go on, put it on."

"In front of you?" Annie clutched the uniform.

"Nothing I ain't seen before. Just strip down to your undergarments."

Annie turned her back and disrobed, squelching her sense of modesty. She donned the yards of fabric and sighed. The skirt stopped a couple inches from the tops of her shoes.

"Don't worry," Mrs. Oakley said. "It's just a matter of taking out the hem. The rest of the dress fits you fine. Take it off, sit a spell, and I'll have you ready by lunchtime."

What had Mother gotten her into? These people were friendlier than a medicine man passing an offering hat. Mother always said folks should stick to their own, but Annie found herself thrust into the middle of a gaggle of women who talked more than they breathed.

After getting dressed, she sat in a chair across from Mrs. Oakley and waited while the woman made the alterations. Sounds of meal preparation reached her from the other side of the door. Dishes clattering, steam hissing, women chattering. Delicious aromas drifted through the cracks, beckoning like presents on Christmas morning.

Annie took a shuddering breath. She didn't have the faintest idea how to act like a lady. Would she find a friend among the other waitresses or be shunned for her tomboyish ways? Most of the town's women seemed to consider Annie a bad influence on their daughters. *Lord, let them like me.*

She stood and opened the door to peek out. A portly man, a young boy and several girls bustled around the modern kitchen like ants, all smiling. Maybe Annie would be happy, too. Regardless, she planned on doing good work. Papa always said any job worth doing was one worth doing right, even if it wasn't your job by choice.

"Here you go." Mrs. Oakley interrupted her thoughts. "Get dressed, make sure to read the hundred and one rules up on the wall." She winked. "And then go find Miss Cartwright. You, Miss Rollins, are going to help tame the West!"

But Annie didn't want to tame the West. She liked it just the way it was.

*

Dallas offered his best friend, Rascal, a sugar cube he had swiped from the kitchen, then rubbed the horse's nose. "The place is filling up, boy. Looks like we might have a group to take sightseeing soon." He turned and leaned against the split railing that made up Rascal's stall. "There's another guide in town, but I heard he's gone a lot. I hope I don't let these people down. The way I figure, you and me might ought to take a ride into the canyon and get familiar with the place after I grab a bite to eat."

With a final pat, he slipped on the jacket he had hung on a nail, and set off toward El Tovar, casting a guilty glance at his new residence. It wasn't that Mrs. Rollins was a bad cook, it was more her sour attitude that turned him away. Something made that woman mighty sad, and while his heart ached for her, he didn't relish eating within sight of her dour countenance if he didn't have to. Besides, he wanted to get a good look at the pretty Harvey Girls. One of them might become Mrs. Baker someday.

His boots clopped across the wide porch of the hotel. He tipped his hat to a couple ladies lounging in rocking chairs, and then pushed through the door. A hostess led him into a dining room way too fancy for the likes of him, dressed as he was in leather britches and a faded shirt.

With a smile, the hostess handed him a dinner jacket. "Dress requirements, sir."

He should have known. Slipping his arms into the too tight garment, he followed the waitress.

"Will this suit you, sir?" The pretty girl smiled and waved a delicate hand toward a table for two.

Dallas caught sight of Annie behind a long wooden bar. "How about over there?"

"The lunch counter? Good choice, sir. Our waitresses make wonderful sandwiches." The hostess turned and led him to a stool at the counter. Dallas could almost make out his reflection in its polished sheen.

"Good morning, Annie." Dallas perched on his seat.

The young woman with Annie whispered something in her ear. Annie turned and smiled. "Good morning, Mr. Baker. Do you have a sandwich preference?" She filled the cup in front of him with coffee.

"Surprise me." He grinned.

"As you surprised me yesterday?" Her eyes flashed.

When would she realize he'd had no idea he was stepping into something she wanted? "Hopefully, the sandwich will leave a better taste in my mouth than my arrival did in yours." He took a sip of his drink.

Annie jerked, dribbling coffee on the countertop. Grabbing a napkin, she bent closer and wiped at the liquid, lowering her voice at the same time. "Let's hope so." She straightened and flashed a grin. "I think a turkey sandwich would suit you fine, since we're fresh out of polecat."

Dallas spurted coffee across the counter, then laughed so hard he thought he'd split a rib. He'd been called many things before but never a turkey, and definitely not by someone with such a pretty smile. "That will be perfect."

From the scowl on the other waitress's face, Dallas figured Annie's remark had been overheard. He hoped she wouldn't get in trouble. After all, she'd said it with a smile, and he had no qualms about sparring with such a pretty gal. Thank goodness she wasn't wearing that split skirt thing. She looked like a regular lady now, even with the high hair.

A train whistle blew. The Harvey Girls snapped to attention, smiles in place, ready to greet the arriving customers. In Dallas's opinion, they put the army to shame the way they lined up at the signal. He turned on the stool to watch the show.

As customers were seated, one waitress filled drinks while another took meal orders. Before he could register what was happening, his coffee was refilled and his sandwich set in front of him. The stools along the counter gradually filled with men.

Annie began at one end of the counter, greeting each man as if he were the only customer in the place, then moved to the next. What would it feel like for her to greet Dallas with the same sincere smile? He'd find out someday, for sure.

The man to his right spoke. "First time here?"

"Yes, you?" Dallas turned back to his lunch.

"Nope. I make a point of stopping every time I'm in the area. The Harvey restaurants are the best along the Santa Fe and have the prettiest waitresses. Some of the girls are married within months of taking the job, but I've got a wife back home. Seeing these lovely ladies makes me miss her." Annie asked if he wanted coffee, and the man nodded.

"I wouldn't mind marrying one of these gals." Dallas took a bite of his sandwich. Fresh turkey, crisp lettuce and well-aged cheese. They didn't skimp on quality, that was for sure.

Annie snorted and moved down the line. Obviously, she didn't agree with his comment.

"That gal there—" the man lifted his cup in her direction "—-s a tall, cool glass of water. Why, I guess she's all of five foot nine. It will take a big man to handle her."

Dallas grinned. The man had no idea how correct he was in this case. "I reckon you're right. She's got a bite for sure."

*

Listen to the men talking, as if she couldn't hear. Annie sniffed. Was that what the restaurant was? A matchmaking service for men looking to get married? Annie wanted to slam down the next man's coffee and dash outside.

She needed to find a way to squelch any notions of marriage. Until she was at least twenty-five. She just needed to convince Mother that her sneaky trick of trying to marry Annie off wasn't going to work. She would most likely have a better chance of roping the moon.

"Hey, pretty lady." The last man in a long line at the counter grinned under a waxed mustache. "Care to keep company later?"

Annie filled his drink. "Thank you, but we aren't allowed to fraternize with customers."

"You look feisty enough to break the rules." He grabbed her hand.

With a tilt of her pitcher, Annie splashed hot coffee across his wrist. The man yelped and pulled away. "Why, you little—"

"I'm terribly sorry, sir. Let me get a cool rag for you." Annie turned, biting her lip to hide her grin.

The man lunged over the counter. "You did that on purpose!"

"You're mistaken." Her heart seized when she saw the glare in his eyes.

He grabbed her arm and pulled her forward. "You owe me a kiss for that little trick."

"That's enough." Dallas grasped the man's shirt collar and yanked him back. "This lady isn't that type of gal. I think you need to leave."

The man looked up at Dallas towering over him. He growled and stormed from the restaurant.

"Thank you." Annie sagged against the counter. "I don't think I can work here if that is going to be the norm."

"It won't."

She stared. "How can you say that, Mr. Baker? You were doing the same thing."

"No, I wasn't." He looked confused.

"Really? You and your friend…" she pointed down

the bar "...were discussing finding brides among the Harvey Girls." She leaned closer across the counter, her nose even with his chin. It was rare to find a man she could literally look up to. My, his eyes sparkled. No, she was furious and wouldn't be sidetracked. "Has it occurred to you that not all women hope to be married as soon as they are out of short skirts?"

"Well, no, I, uh, well, I thought all women wanted to be married."

"Someday, perhaps, Mr. Baker." Annie took a deep breath, ready to let loose another string of words. "But not yet."

"Back to work, Miss Rollins." The head waitress tapped her shoulder. "Thank you, sir, for coming to the aid of one of our girls."

"It's my pleasure, ma'am." Dallas nodded and left the dining room.

Annie took a deep breath, pasted on the required smile, and got back to work. She could assess her feelings and attraction for the man who'd stolen her dreams later.

3

Dallas gave Rascal his head and let the horse pick his way down the steep trail into the canyon. Thank goodness his sturdy horse was used to climbing in and out of gorges. Allowing the horse free rein gave Dallas time to organize his thoughts regarding Annie and her views on marriage.

Had he been as bad as the man who'd accosted her? He still found it hard to believe that the lovely gal didn't want to get married. Ever since they were out of pigtails, his sisters had thought of little else. They'd known the color of dress they wanted to wear years before they were old enough to wed, or had a man snagged.

The horse stumbled on loose rocks, almost going to its knees and waking Dallas from his daydreams. He glanced over his shoulder to see how far they'd come.

A woman's silhouette stood outlined on the canyon's

rim. Dallas smiled. No one needed to tell him who watched from above. If he were closer, he'd wager steam came from her ears at her inability to follow. He actually looked forward to the next time he could get into a verbal sparring match with Annie. She might not want to marry, but she was great fun, nevertheless.

A cottontail darted in front of the horse. Rascal hopped, coming too close to the edge of the trail for Dallas's comfort. If they fell, it was a long way down. Once they got to the canyon floor, they could both breathe easier.

The sun hung high overhead by the time they reached bottom. Dallas removed his hat, hoping to catch a breeze. Rascal headed straight for the river. Dallas wouldn't mind a drink of cool water himself. It might be a mite chilly at times on the rim, but down in the canyon the sun beat with ferocity on his head and shoulders. He shook his canteen. Half-full.

He dismounted by the river's edge and dipped his bandanna in the cool water of the Colorado. Closing his eyes, he wiped his face before standing, and let the water soak the neckline of his shirt.

"Hold it right there, mister." A low, gravelly voice and the distinct sound of a gun being cocked apprised Dallas of the stranger's intentions.

He held up his hands, bandanna dangling from his fingers, and took his time turning. "Can I help you with something?"

The wiry man in front of him looked as if he'd baked under the sun for years. "You can get back on your horse and skedaddle. This is my spot."

"I'm afraid you're wrong there."

The man poked Dallas in the chest with the barrel of

his gun. "I said git! Any gold here is mine, and I'll shoot the man that says otherwise."

How was Dallas supposed to lead visitors to the canyon for camping trips if there would be a threat of danger such as a man gone loco? "It's a big river. Can't you move to a different spot farther upstream?"

The man narrowed his eyes and tilted his head to the side. "No, I don't reckon I can."

Dallas sighed. "Look. I've been hired to lead tourists into the canyon. In a few weeks, there will be a lot more folks down here than just me. I'm suggesting you move for that reason and no other." He figured the chance of finding gold in a river was slim to none, and the old coot had as a good a chance in a different location. "Unless you move away from the hotels, you're going to be bothered quite a bit. There's a promising bunch of rocks down the river that might yield you some color."

The man lowered his weapon and frowned. "I reckon you're right. I ain't had much luck in this spot, anyway." He grabbed the reins to a swaybacked mule and meandered off.

One more reason why a male tour guide was the wisest choice. Dallas hated to think what might have happened had Annie been caught alone. With her sharp tongue, she might not have been able to talk the man out of shooting her. Dallas chuckled. Most likely, the old coot would have shot her just to make her stop talking.

The area a few feet from the water looked smooth enough to pitch some tents. All he'd need to do was move a few rocks to make the ground less uncomfortable. They could use the stones to form a fire pit. As he paced the riverbank, he envisioned the campsite in his mind. Women's tents on one side, men's on the other. Mules could be tethered over there. A heavy rain would derail things a bit if people were caught in a downpour, but even that could be withstood by moving the tourists under an overhang if they were caught unaware.

How many times did Mrs. Rollins intend him to guide people? Once a week? Twice? All year? The place would look mighty pretty covered with snow.

He leaned back and popped the kinks from his spine. Winter in the canyon would sure be something to look at. Guess there were quite a few questions he needed answers to. Too bad he couldn't ask the pretty Annie.

He could imagine how that conversation would go. Probably as well as rain on the Fourth of July. He whistled for Rascal to follow, then continued his stroll along the river's edge, noting places of interest and those where a person might find trouble. Yes, sir. Women were not meant to be trail guides. There were way too many problems to figure out, and women just weren't made that way.

*

The next morning, Annie kicked a rock over the lip of the canyon. What was taking that man so long to return? She had a million questions about what it looked like down there.

Smoothing the black fabric of her uniform firmly across her backside, she plopped on her favorite fallen log and prepared to wait. With supper served, and Mother reclining from a headache, Annie had plenty of time to waste waiting for the scoundrel who'd taken her dream away. She sighed and leaned forward, elbows resting on her knees.

Maybe she didn't have her facts completely accurate. Mother never did say she'd agreed to let her be the tour guide, but it was definitely Annie's idea. No dispute there!

The rattle of rocks alerted her to Dallas's presence before the horse's head came into view. Annie popped to her feet and patted her hair into place before trotting alongside the horse.

"What's it like down there? Is it as beautiful as I imagine? You were gone forever."

"It's quite a ways down." Dallas's eyes glittered in the fading light. "I don't have any idea what you imagine, but I'd say it looks like the desert, painted brown, mauve, terracotta, and with bits of green mixed in."

"Brown?" Her nose wrinkled.

"Yep, from cactus and sage. The river is swift and it winds a lot as it runs through the canyon." He slid from the horse and looped the reins over his shoulder. "Want me to take you sometime?"

Did she? Would that be admitting defeat? "No, thank you. I'll go myself soon. Was it pretty? You didn't say anything about the awesome beauty of the canyon. Why is it that men leave out the more decorative details?"

"Really? I did describe the colors. Besides, I'm looking at something mighty pretty right now."

Annie glanced around them. "What are you looking at? It's the same every day. A dirt street, a towering hotel. No, the only thing with any beauty is the canyon."

"I disagree. Besides, it's quite dangerous—and, well, doesn't your job take up a lot of your time?"

She narrowed her eyes, not missing his abrupt

change of topic. "My job is not my life or what I intend to do for the rest of my life. My job is something I do to placate my mother until something else comes along."

"That's commendable." His mouth quirked.

"Are you being facetious?" He really knew how to get under her skin.

"A bit." He stopped and faced her. "Sure, you're working at the restaurant to make your mother happy, but who does that really help, Annie? Not you or the restaurant. Definitely not your mother."

"That is none of your concern." She planted her fists on her hips. "I'm sure you would be more than happy for a woman to sit at home and do nothing."

"I doubt that would happen. My ma and sisters always seem to have plenty of work to do."

Annie stamped her foot. "You are incorrigible. I pity the woman who ever marries you." Hitching her skirts, she dashed into the house, ran up the stairs and then slammed the door to her room. The man was a cad.

It was the twentieth century. Women were capable of more than doing laundry and having babies. She threw herself across the mattress. So what if she took a job to help her mother. They'd both been through enough. She rolled over, then grunted when the knot from her apron dug into her back. Silly uniform.

She sat up, untied the apron, then tossed it across the room onto the rocking chair. Working at El Tovar wasn't her choice, but she'd do a fine job regardless. Who was Dallas to say otherwise?

A knock sounded at the door. "Annette? I baked some scones today. Would you come join me?"

"Yes, Mother. Let me change out of my uniform." Annie straightened and changed into a simple cotton day dress. It was good that her mother interrupted her wayward thoughts. Dallas Baker occupied them way too much.

Simply because he took away her dreams, she admitted, nothing else. But the man created a fine picture on the back of his horse.

Mother sat at their old wood table in the kitchen, two steaming cups of coffee and a plate of strawberry scones in front of her. She smiled and gestured to the chair across from her. "This is nice. I missed you today."

"I'm exhausted." Annie took her seat and accepted the cup her mother slid toward her. "I missed being home, also. The men who frequent the restaurant seem to think it's a place to find a wife."

"Really?" Her mother's eyes lit up.

"Mother." Annie took her time taking a bite of scone and a sip of coffee, choosing her words carefully. "I am not in a hurry to marry."

"But you're nineteen years old! I had you at that age and had already been married for three years."

"Times have changed. A modern woman doesn't rush into marriage."

"Posh." Her mother set her cup down hard enough to slosh her drink over the rim. "Daughter, with your good looks and moral upbringing, you are in high demand. Especially here in Williams. But—" she raised her eyebrows "—even you shouldn't be too picky. You stand in danger of becoming an old maid. I won't be around forever, and you'll be alone."

"You're not even forty years old." Annie ran her gaze over her mother's chestnut hair and wrinkle free skin. "You could still marry, if you felt inclined."

"No." Tears shimmered in her eyes. "I'm not desirable anymore."

"Mother." Annie reached across the table and laid a hand over hers. "If you dislike Williams so much, why don't you go back East? Visit your sister for a while. I can manage fine on my own."

Mother reached for a napkin and dabbed her eyes. "No, it wouldn't be proper for you to be alone."

"But you would consider taking a holiday if I weren't alone?"

"We have boarders, Annette. Stop being ridiculous. I have way too much work to do to consider such a thing." Her mother straightened. The usual determined gleam returned to her eyes. "Drink your coffee before it gets cold."

What had happened? Annie sat back. For a moment, she'd caught a glimpse of the mother she'd had before her father's death. Then a curtain fell, blocking out that woman, and replacing her with the one in front of Annie. Did it make her a horrible daughter to want the kind, gentle version back?

Annie froze, the scone halfway to her mouth. For the first time in her life, her mother had commented favorably on her looks. So had Dallas.

The pretty thing he had spoken about…was her.

4

Annie tried to stroll in a ladylike manner toward the hotel, instead of shuffling as Dallas led a group of six men and two women on mules past the boardinghouse and over the lip of the canyon. Oh, life was so unfair. She kicked at a rock, scuffing her shoe. She'd have to repolish that spot before beginning work, or receive a demerit.

She stopped before climbing the hotel stairs, and cast another glance toward the canyon. One look wouldn't hurt anything. She'd barely be tardy. Hitching up her skirt, she dashed in the direction Dallas and his guests had disappeared. They'd be gone for three days. It wouldn't hurt to wave goodbye.

Stopping at the top of the trail with enough abruptness to send pebbles cascading over the side, Annie lifted her right hand to shade her eyes. There. Around the curve she could make out Dallas leading the line. Old man Horace, the other guide, wouldn't be far behind.

She waved. A grin spread across her face as Dallas waved his hat in her direction. She so wanted to be there, second in line if not first. A woman to converse with the two women guests making the trip.

Her shoulders slumped as she turned back to her job. She entered through the back door just as the train whistle blew. Oh, my. She dashed to Mrs. Oakley's room and grabbed a polishing cloth. After a quick swipe at her shoe, she rushed to the lunch counter, took position and pasted a smile to her face.

"Cutting it close, aren't we?" Dottie, the other lunch girl, seemed to have a personal vendetta against Annie since the first day. "It wouldn't do for Miss Cartwright to find out."

"Mind your own business." Annie moved farther down the counter. Anywhere was better than right next to the spiteful redhead.

Soon, the counter filled with hungry customers, and Annie hopped to get them served. Once a train arrived, there was little time for petty grievances or wishing she was somewhere else. Because El Tovar was a hotel, the serving didn't stop when the train pulled out. Most nights, Annie made her way home long past dark.

It wasn't that she didn't like her job. She did, surprisingly enough, other than the lack of freedom to spend outdoors. There were most likely worse jobs for women. Most of the girls were friendly, and Miss Cartwright was one of the sweetest women Annie had ever met, but there was the occasional bad apple. In the month that she had worked for the Fred Harvey Company, Dottie seemed to have a mysterious grudge against her.

Keeping a smile on her face, Annie wiped spilled coffee from the polished counter after the customers left. The question was, why did Dottie dislike her? They'd never laid eyes on each other until Annie's employment.

"Look sharp, ladies." Miss Cartwright pulled a pocket watch from her apron pocket. "The train is late, and the passengers will be in a hurry."

Annie stashed the rag under the counter and stood at attention as the train pulled into the station. She couldn't explain why, but the moment the doors opened and the people crowded inside was her favorite part. She loved the eager looks on their faces, knowing they would receive a meal equal to big city restaurants. Yes, Annie still yearned to explore the canyon floor, but here in El Tovar she could live, temporarily, through the adventures of others.

Three men, dusty under the borrowed jackets the hotel's dress code required, sat at Annie's end of the bar. All three ordered coffee and ham sandwiches. And all three watched every move she made.

Her skin prickled under their scrutiny. Most of the dining guests were friendly, but these men had yet to crack a smile.

By the time they'd eaten and had their second cups of coffee, the train was preparing to pull out of the station, and still the men sat. Obviously they intended to stay in town awhile longer. Annie wasn't sure why the idea made her nervous, but instinct warned their visit would not be pleasant for someone.

"Pa, this hotel is a bit fancy for my taste." A man in his twenties plunked down his cup. "This jacket they gave us is constricting."

"Stop bellyaching," the older man said. "Your ma taught you better than that. Miss?"

Annie paused in clearing away their dishes. "Yes, sir?"

"Is there another place to stay besides the El Tovar? Seems my boys have an aversion to luxury."

"The Rollins Boardinghouse is right down the road. Feels more like home." And her mother could use the income. Still, there was something about these three that didn't sit right with Annie. She prayed she wasn't sending danger to her mother's doorstep.

"One more question, if you've the time." The older gentleman wiped his mouth with his napkin, then tossed the white cloth on the counter. "I'm looking for a man by the name of Dallas Baker. You wouldn't happen to know of him, would you?"

*

Dallas tethered Rascal in a patch of grass, then moved to stir the coals in order to start coffee for breakfast. A simple meal of hardtack and bacon would suffice.

From the smiles and murmurs coming from his guests, he deduced the trips since he'd arrived in Williams weeks ago had been a success. He'd no sooner arrive back at the boardinghouse then it was time to take out another group. This time, after three days, he was more than eager to return to the Rollinses'. A bedroll on the ground was no match for a soft mattress, and his coffee was nowhere near as good as Mrs. Rollins's.

A hawk soared overhead, its cries serving as an alarm for whoever still dozed in their tents. Hard ground at night or not, Dallas thanked God for the opportunity to spend his days in the great outdoors, and a homey place to rest his head once in a while. The bird swooped and emerged with a squealing mouse in his talons.

"Beautiful morning. I thought the rain last night would wash us away." Mr. Wood, one of the trail guests, hunkered on the opposite side of the fire. "I contemplated booking the tour with the El Tovar because of the hotel's prestige and luxury, but the smaller group you led allowed for a more personal experience."

"I'm glad you enjoyed it, sir." Dallas set the coffeepot next to the glowing coals.

The man nodded. "I'll inform my acquaintances of the Rollins trail guides. You and the old man should also consider longer tours. Maybe a week of following the river."

"We'll definitely take that into consideration." Dallas glanced at the riverbank, where Horace was instructing one of the guests on the best way to fish. He couldn't wait to tell Annie that her idea of drawing guests to her family's business was a success, at least the tour part. Now, if she could only find a way to draw overnight guests away from El Tovar.

Would she be pleased or upset that he was the one to hear the man's praises? Dallas hoped she would be happy, but as the one who'd taken what she had hoped would be her job, he feared she'd be angry.

By midmorning, the group began their trek back up the narrow trail to the canyon's rim. With the previous night's rain, the trail was more dangerous than usual, and Dallas looked behind him more than he did to the trail ahead. If he'd had his way, he would have liked to camp an extra night to let the ground dry some, but the guests had voted to go on. All he could do now was pray and be vigilant.

Rascal's left hind leg slipped on loose rocks. He snorted and tossed his mane. Dallas's heart shot to his throat. "Let your mule have its head," he called behind him. "They know the safest place to set their feet. Horace, keep a lookout back there."

Horace waved his hat to let Dallas know he'd heard.

"I'm terrified, Mr. Baker." Mrs. Romero, one of the female guests, clutched at the lace around her throat. "My beast is sliding around something terrible. It's a long way down. Maybe we should go back."

Dallas clamped his lips together. She'd thrown the biggest fit over an extra night's stay in the wilderness. "No, ma'am. There's no safe place to turn around. We keep moving forward." Next time, he'd use his status as guide and put his foot down. Safety didn't come by majority rule.

He continued to pray for safety as they made their way, step by step, toward the rim. The two pack mules at the end of the line brayed. He didn't blame them. Fear had set up residence in his gut, too. Perspiration broke out on his upper lip. What a fool he was to allow himself to be coerced into a trip he knew was dangerous. But then, Horace was the experienced one of the two, and he hadn't said anything against going. "Hold 'em steady, folks."

"One of those mules is bucking something fierce back here," one of the guests yelled. "He's spooking my mount. The old man is having a hard time controlling them."

Dallas urged Rascal a bit faster. If he remembered

correctly, there was a small area near the canyon wall ahead where he could stop and let the others pass. That way, he could grab the lead ropes to the mules and calm them. One big slip and they might lose more than an animal.

It was plumb foolishness for Annie to think she could lead tours. What if she encountered a situation like the present one? Would she be calm enough of mind and wits to get the party to safety? Most of the women he knew tended to show hysterics at the first sign of danger, much like the increasing agitation of the two women with the group today. Their voices continued to rise in volume, and they shrieked with each rattle of loose rocks. He hated to think of what could happen if one of them lost her head.

Finding the spot he'd searched for, he crowded Rascal against the rock and waved the others forward. Once they'd passed, he reached out and grabbed for the first pack mule's lead rope. The animal shied away.

"Whoa, boy." Dallas slid from the back of his horse. He waved for Horace to continue on, while he worked to calm the animal.

"Okay, Baker," Horace said. "I've separated the two in order to settle them down, but that one acts like he's got a burr under his blanket."

"Mr. Baker, do you think it wise to stay behind alone?" Mrs. Romero's dark eyes widened as she glanced back at him.

"Continue to the top, ma'am. I have everything here under control." No sense in letting the others think otherwise. Especially since he was in danger of plummeting several hundred feet to his death.

"Come on, boy." He inched forward. His fingers

brushed the rope, then grabbed hold.

The mule stepped back, slid, and fought to gain a firm footing. The rope slipped through Dallas's hands. He hissed at the burn and let go. The mule screamed and disappeared.

Dallas plastered his back against the rock wall. Thank God there hadn't been anyone riding the animal. His heart sank as the mule's cries faded, then stopped. The other one stood still, head hanging. Dallas took the rope and led the animal back to Rascal. Usually, he'd loop the rope around the saddle horn, but not this time. He wouldn't risk the life of his friend.

The others reached the top several minutes before he did. When his head cleared the rim, Annie ran toward him. "Mr. Baker! Are you all right? The others told us of the accident. Were you frightened? Thank goodness you let go."

Despite her obvious concern for his safety, Dallas detected a trace of excitement in her voice. The trail was definitely not a place for Annie Rollins. "I'm fine, Miss Rollins, thank you." They'd got past the formality of last names a while ago, but had decided to continue to use them while around the guests.

She leaned close and lowered her voice. "There are three men here looking for you. They've checked into the boardinghouse."

"Hello, son."

Dallas stared into the faces of his pa and older brothers.

5

His pa? Annie trotted along behind the long-legged men as they headed back to the boardinghouse.

Dallas stopped. "I've got to see to the horse and mules. Miss Rollins, please make sure the guests make their way back to the El Tovar."

"Of course." Annie stopped, taken aback. Why didn't he look pleased to be reunited with his family? They seem to have come a long way. She fell into step behind the tour guests.

"I hope your ride was pleasant."

"Oh, my, yes," one of the women said. "Fraught with danger, beautiful scenery, a multitude of wildlife, and Mr. Baker was a true gentleman the entire time. I was most comfortable, considering the surroundings."

Annie stifled a sigh. The whole thing sounded too exciting to be true. How she would love a bit of danger in her life. Nothing deadly, of course, but something to get the blood pumping. Something more than helping Mother make beds, or serving customers at the fancy hotel that was seriously affecting her mother's livelihood.

"Do you work at the El Tovar?" The woman creased her brow. "It certainly seemed as if you worked at the Rollins place."

"My mother owns the boardinghouse next to the canyon, and yes, I work for the Harvey Company." Until now, it hadn't registered exactly how odd that might appear to a stranger. She smoothed the fabric of her dress, wishing she'd taken the time to change. But when she'd gotten off work and Dallas and the group hadn't returned, she'd stood watch on the rim, not thinking at all about changing out of her uniform.

Once the guests were on the massive hotel porch, Annie lifted her skirts and sprinted home. She couldn't care less if anyone saw and reported her unladylike behavior to Mother. Soon, Dallas would meet with his family in the parlor, and she didn't want to miss a thing.

She barreled through the front door, past the dining room where the Baker family sat, past her mother's shocked expression, and thundered up the stairs. Before she closed her bedroom door, she heard soft footfalls on the steps.

"Annette Rollins! Have you lost your mind?" Mother glared down her nose. "We have guests. What will they think of such behavior from a young woman?"

"That I'm spirited?" She reached behind her for the buttons running down her back.

"Impertinent. Impetuous. Irresponsible. Take your pick." Mother moved to help her. "Why such a rush?"

"Because Dallas's family is here. He doesn't seem

happy to see them."

"You're sticking your nose where it doesn't belong."

Annie grinned at her reflection in the mirror. "Yes, I suppose I am."

Mother sighed. "You and your zest for adventure will be the death of me."

Her uniform puddled around her ankles and she stepped clear of the pile. Grabbing a day dress from a nearby peg, she slipped it over her head while Mother hung up the uniform. Annie supposed she did test her mother's patience on a regular basis, but God hadn't created her to sit back while others enjoyed life. If some of her love of adventure could rub off on her mother, life would be much easier.

Annie removed the pins from what was left of her pompadour and quickly weaved her hair into a braid. The sound of the front door banging alerted her that Dallas had returned. "Come on, Mother." She whirled and dashed down the stairs, skidding to a halt at the dining room doorway.

If the men stayed around the table, it would be much easier to eavesdrop without being obvious. She avoided Dallas's gaze. "May I fetch you gentlemen something to eat? It won't take but a minute to make up some sandwiches and brew a pot of coffee. And we have lemonade."

"That sounds mighty fine, young lady," the older gentleman said.

Dallas blew air sharply out of his nose. "Annie, this is my father, Frank Baker, and my brothers, Dalton and Conway."

"We're his older brothers," Dalton, the one with a mustache, pointed out. "He's the baby." He grinned.

"That's enough." Dallas plopped into a chair.

"I'm pleased to meet you. All of you." Annie smiled and hurried into the kitchen. She would be able to hear perfectly fine from in there as long as Mother didn't bang the dishes. She glared as two tin plates fell onto the counter.

Mother gave a thin smile. "I know exactly what you're doing, tiptoeing around like a cat. Well, you were brought up better. I will not let you listen in on a private conversation."

"Aren't you in the least bit interested?" Surely, if they wanted their talk to be private, they would've gone outside. "Perhaps I'll be able to help them mend their differences."

"Meddle in their affairs, more likely." Mother removed a chunk of butter from the cooler. "You don't even care for Dallas."

Annie paused. She rarely saw their handsome trail guide. She'd been concerned about his late return. That meant she cared for him, correct? But how much? As a friend? Employee? Or did her interest in his life mean something more? She put a hand to her throat. Goodness. She did seem overly concerned about the man, didn't she?

Mother filled glasses with fresh squeezed lemonade. "That quieted you." She carried the tray out of the kitchen.

Rarely at a loss for words, Annie found herself stumped. She had hardly spent any time with Dallas. How could she be so attracted to him? The idea was inconceivable. They passed in the morning and sometimes in the evening, offering each other nothing more than a "Good morning" or "Have a good evening." Neither of which were the basis for a relationship. It wasn't even enough for a friendship.

What was wrong with her? When had her anger at him for taking away her job turned to appreciation?

*

"Why are you here?" Dallas straightened and fixed a glare on his father as Mrs. Rollins set glasses of lemonade on the table. He hated gracing her table while dirty from the trail, but the sight of his family sent all thoughts of cleaning to the back of his mind.

"To bring you home." Pa grabbed a sandwich off the plate Annie set on the table.

She gasped and took a step back. Most likely she was wondering how she could take over as trail guide if Dallas left. Remorse burned through him. He wasn't being fair. There was no need to get petty with her because of his annoyance with his family. He shook his head and stared at the thick ham sandwich in front of him, all appetite gone. "I'm not going back."

"Look." Dalton folded his arms on the table. "We understand your need for independence, but the family stays together. Can't you lead rich city folk around our own land?"

"It isn't the Grand Canyon."

"No, it's the great state of Texas." Conway pounded the table. "You're breaking Ma's heart."

Dallas crossed his arms and leaned back in the chair, balancing on the back legs. "Ma is the one who encouraged me to come."

"That right?" Pa raised an eyebrow. "You're not joshin'?"

"No, sir. Ma told me to follow my dream. Where do you think I got the money?"

"All four legs on the floor." Mrs. Rollins refilled their lemonade. "Annie, fetch the cake on the counter, please."

A couple minutes later, while Dallas still stared at the three other Baker men, Annie plopped a coconut cake in the center of the table. His throat threatened to seize. It looked just like the ones Ma made. He missed her something terrible, but didn't relish being bossed around by his brothers. Either they took him on as a partner on the ranch or they could run it without him.

"You're as stubborn as your ma," Pa said, shaking his head. "Why'd you feel such a need to go?"

"I don't want to be a hired hand. It's a partner or nothing."

"You have to prove yourself, same as we did," Dalton said. "We all started as cowhands."

"I am proving myself." Dallas lifted his sandwich to his mouth. Old habits died hard and if he wanted a piece of that cake, he needed to eat his supper first. "Just not in the way you think I should."

"You lost a mule today, son." Pa gave a sideways glance at Mrs. Rollins. "Which he'll pay you back for, ma'am."

She nodded and started slicing the cake. "In due time."

"He might've lost a mule," Annie said, pulling up another chair, "but according to the folks who were with him, he could've lost his life. Or one of theirs. They had nothing but glowing recommendations about your son's abilities as trail guide. In fact, they intend to spread the word about his abilities."

"Young lady, my son should never have led those people up that trail after a hard rain."

Annie lifted her chin. Dallas put a hand over hers to still her. "The paying customers voted. It won't happen again."

"Gentlemen, while this conversation is intriguing, it is personal, and the hour is growing late. May I suggest you check in, either here or at the hotel, and continue in the morning, when everyone is level-headed?" Mrs. Rollins smiled around the room. "Or you may feel free to discuss the issue in the parlor." She rested a hand on Dallas's shoulder. "As for this young man's talents in leading our customers, I believe he did a fine job and is an asset to this establishment. I would hate to see him leave us. Good evening, gentlemen. Dallas, if your family chooses to stay, any available room is open to them. Annie, follow me."

She glided from the room, leaving them in silence. His brothers ducked their heads and dug into their slices of cake. Dallas finished his sandwich, then stood. "I'll show y'all to your rooms and you can settle up in the morning."

"I suppose it's for the best." Pa stood and clapped him on the shoulder. "Think it over, son. Your place on the ranch will always be there. I'll give your ma your love."

"Does that mean I can stay without any argument?" Could it be that easy? He should have stood up for himself years ago.

"For now." Pa grinned. "I'm worn-out. Show me where I can rest my weary bones. Your brothers can share a room."

By the time Dallas made it to his own room on the third floor, exhaustion weighed him so much he could barely toe off his boots. The pitcher of clear water on the bureau taunted him. There was no way he could slide between Mrs. Rollins's clean sheets without washing off the dust. He disrobed down to his underclothes.

Using a rag left folded on the top, he scrubbed his face and arms with water grown cool, his mind running over the day's and night's events. It was surprising how Annie had stood up for him against his family. Had he pegged her wrong? Maybe she wasn't as upset at him as he'd thought. Or maybe…his spirit brightened…being a Harvey Girl was turning Annie into a regular lady.

One who knew her place in the world and was ready to leave the line between men and women's roles intact. He dropped the rag into the water. If so, then maybe he could spend a little time dwelling on how pretty she was and how much he enjoyed their greetings in the mornings.

He pulled back the blankets and lay down. What would she say if he invited her for a picnic on Sunday? They could take things nice and slow, getting to be friends first. After all, she still had over five months of her contract left. Then, if Annie Rollins was the woman God intended to be Dallas's bride, he'd pack her up and take her home to Ma.

6

Annie tied her uniform apron around her waist, making sure the bow was as perfect as possible, then hurried down the stairs in hopes the Baker men were still around. Mother had scooted her away before their conversation had been complete. What if she'd missed something important?

Her hand stilled on the stair banister. Important? What could they possibly have to say that would be important enough for her to hear their private business? She sat on the step. Was she so lonely for news of what went on outside Williams that she had reverted to sticking her nose where it didn't belong? She clutched her throat. She'd turned into a nosy woman!

"What in heaven's name are you doing sitting on the stairs?" Mother bustled by with an armload of napkins to be folded. "If you have time to dawdle before work, you have time to help me."

"I'm coming." She pushed to her feet and followed her mother into the dining room.

The Baker men sat around the table nursing coffee and exclaiming over mother's morning pastries. One glance at the clock told Annie time was speeding by and she would be late for work if she didn't hurry.

She grabbed a cinnamon roll and poured a cup of coffee. "Good morning, gentlemen." They seemed less tense. Obviously, they'd settled something the night before.

Mother hissed from the kitchen door. "Annie."

"What?" She moved to her side.

"We do not eat with our guests."

"I'm running late, and I'm sure they won't mind." She stood in the doorway and listened to them rave over the rolls. "Mother, I have another idea."

Mother sighed. "Of course you do."

"You work too hard, and since you've found employment for me somewhere else, I'm thinking maybe you should offer only breakfast to your guests, and run a bakery instead of cooking all the meals." Her mind raced with ideas, but they needed to be discussed with other parties before approaching her mother. "I'm taking a plate of these rolls to the El Tovar. It's part of my plan." Annie lifted the tray.

"What are you prattling on about?" Mother's hands flew as she folded napkins. The hotel could definitely use a woman of her skill, if she ever gave up the boardinghouse.

"This is called a bed-and-*breakfast* boardinghouse for a reason," Annie explained. "Make it one."

"If I don't serve meals, the guests will buy them from the hotel." Mother shook her head. "It won't work."

"I'm not finished digging through all the details." Annie planted a quick kiss on her cheek. "Trust me." She grinned, hefted the tray on her shoulder and left through the back door. She'd find a way of keeping the boardinghouse going if it killed her.

She pushed through the back entrance to the hotel kitchen and set the tray on the counter. The chef, Richard Swanson, and the hotel manager, Harold Lawrence, were inside, taking a moment to enjoy hot cups of coffee.

"Gentlemen," Annie said. "I have a treat to go with that coffee."

"What's this?" Mr. Lawrence peered at the pastries. "Not from the hotel, are they?"

"No, sir. My mother made them." Annie folded her hands and took a step back, waiting for the men's reactions.

They each bit into one. Mr. Lawrence's eyes . "Heaven. Your mother, you say?"

Mr. Swanson took three bites before speaking. "I cannot bake this well. Why did you bring these? To tease me?"

"No, sir. I have a proposition for the two of you." Annie grinned. "The hotel is taking away my mother's business at the boardinghouse. As you can see, she is a wonderful baker. I'm suggesting an arrangement beneficial to both parties. The El Tovar pays my mother to supply pastries for the hotel. She can make different baked items for each meal, as long as an order is given the day before."

The men glanced at each other. "I like it," Mr. Lawrence said. "Very much."

"Me, too." The chef wiped his hands on his apron. "It

would give me time to concentrate on the entrées.

"It's a deal," Mr. Lawrence said. "When do we start?"

Annie chuckled. "I need to approach my mother with the idea. I'll let you know tomorrow."

"Very well. I will want dinner rolls and pastries for Friday. We will start then." Mr. Swanson waved his hands. "Now, out of my kitchen. Leave the pastries with me."

Her steps light, Annie floated to the lunch counter and started rolling silverware in napkins. She smiled, thinking of her mother doing the same thing. Mother couldn't help but be pleased when Annie approached her with the final plans. Now, she needed to come up with an idea to actually draw guests to the boardinghouse.

Of course, Mother charged less than the hotel, but now wouldn't offer three square meals. The canyon tours were drawing guests for that aspect of the business, but it wasn't putting folks' heads on Mother's fresh pillowcases at night. Annie needed to come up with something the hotel couldn't offer.

Something original, like what Fred Harvey did when he saw a need for good food and service along the railroad. Something only Annie and Mother could offer a guest.

She was so engrossed in her thoughts that Dottie elbowed her when the breakfast guests crowded into the room. "Wake up. I'm not working this entire counter alone." Her smile never faltered while she spat out the words.

Annie slid the unfolded napkins and silverware under the counter, and snapped to attention. It wouldn't do to daydream while at work. Waitressing might not have been her first choice of employment, but now that she was there, she intended to give it her best. At least until Mother realized that finding a husband would not come as a result of working in the Harvey Company.

Tame the West, indeed. Annie would like to tame the next man who offered her marriage, with a cast-iron skillet against his hard head. Maybe that was a bit drastic, but unlike several of the other girls, she was not looking for a husband.

Life had too much to offer a young unmarried woman, and Annie intended to enjoy it all before settling down. Her gaze landed on Dallas, coming through the door. Even if one of the prospects was more pleasing to the eye than a bald eagle soaring over her beloved canyon.

*

Dallas planted himself on a stool at the lunch counter and watched Annie serve customers while he nursed a cup of coffee and thought over the morning's conversation with his family. They'd finally agreed to give him a year to get independence out of his system. He shook his head.

Sure, he loved his family's ranch, but he would stick to his guns about becoming a partner or not returning. His brothers hadn't had to prove themselves, so why should he? It wasn't that he was irresponsible...well, maybe running off the way he had was irresponsible...but sometimes it took a man doing something drastic before his family would listen. Ma understood. Why couldn't the others?

"More coffee?" Annie's question jerked him from his thoughts.

"Uh, yeah. Sorry."

"You look like your mind is miles away."

"It is." He folded his arms on the counter. "If anyone can understand my dilemma, it'll be you. Do you have a moment?"

She glanced at the other waitress, who cocked her head. "No. I'm sorry, I don't. But why don't I meet you on my mother's porch when I return home?"

"That'll do." He needed to check over the gear used in yesterday's tour. That would keep him plenty busy until Annie returned home. He plunked down the change for his coffee and headed back outside.

The afternoon sun beat on his head, shouting to the world that summer was coming with a vengeance. Still, Dallas doubted the heat could rival that of his hometown. He plopped his hat on his head and sauntered toward the Rollins barn.

By the time he'd finished, and settled in one of the porch rockers to wait on Annie, night had begun its descent. He didn't wait long before he saw her hurrying up the walk, carrying a silver tray.

"Let me give this back to my mother, and I'll be right out." The screen banged shut behind her.

"Must you always slam the door?" Mrs. Rollins's strident voice carried to his ears.

"Sorry. How do you feel about baking for the hotel?"

"Why in the world would I do that?"

"For the money, of course." Annie's words dripped with frustration. "They'll pay you well. They'll place an order each day for what they need in two days. This way, you only need to serve breakfast to your guests. You can spend the rest of the day baking, and make more money doing so. I also have another idea."

Dallas chuckled at the sigh emanating from Mrs. Rollins. He didn't mean to eavesdrop, but considering his position on the porch, and the open windows, he couldn't do much else.

"We need incentives to pull guests from the El Tovar. Since you hired a trail guide, we can offer free tours with a three-night stay. I'm sure more ideas will come to me as time passes."

"I'm sure they will." Mrs. Rollins paused for a moment. "These are actually very good ideas, Annie. You've always had a good mind for organization and creativity. You may tell the hotel that I accept their offer of baking. I may even hire a girl to help me."

"That's wonderful." Minutes later, Annie sat in the rocking chair next to Dallas. "Since the window is open, I'm sure you heard our conversation."

"I did. My apologies."

She waved his words away. "No need. If it were private, Mother would've closed the window. Now…" Annie turned to look at him. "What did you want to discuss with me?"

"I just needed someone to express my frustration to. The notion is gone now."

"Nonsense. You said I would understand, if anyone would."

Dallas took a deep breath. "True. My family is upset with me for leaving our ranch in Texas and coming here to Arizona. While ranching is nice, and I do want to do it someday, I want an adventure first. I need to prove that I'm more than the younger brother. Does that make sense?"

"Very much." She leaned back against the wood slats of the rocker. "You crave adventure as much as I do."

She stared toward the canyon. "I still intend to go to the bottom, you know. Mother thinks I'll find a husband working at the El Tovar. So many girls do. But not me."

"Do you ever intend to marry?" He held his breath while he waited for her to answer. He didn't think an adventurous wife would suit him, but every girl settled down eventually, didn't she?"

She shrugged. "Someday. Maybe." She returned her attention to him. "What kind of agreement did you arrive at with your family?"

"They gave me a year to make up my mind what I want to do." He leaned his head back. "I have every intention of returning, but it has to be on my terms. No more browbeating from my brothers."

"Well, as an only child, I can't say I understand how that feels. But..." she paused and lowered her voice "...I do know what it feels like to have someone else make your decisions for you."

"Annette! It's much too late for you to be sitting unchaperoned, in the dark, on the porch." Mrs. Rollins stood on the other side of the screen door.

"Coming." Annie stood. She stopped and leaned to whisper in Dallas's ear. "I think my mother is the one who needs a husband. Then she'd have someone to boss around other than me."

Dallas laughed as she stormed inside. Whoever married Annie Rollins would have his hands full. He turned and caught a glimpse of her back before she disappeared up the stairs. Maybe that wouldn't be a bad thing, after all.

7

Finally, a day off from work at the hotel. Instead of attending church with her mother, Annie donned her split skirt and took her Bible to her favorite spot overlooking the canyon. A person couldn't get any closer to God than in the middle of His creation.

Annie flipped through the pages to Psalms. *"I will praise You because I am fearfully and wonderfully made; Your works are wonderful, I know that full well."* She ran her finger over the words, then gazed across the great expanse in front of her.

God had made her the way she was. He'd given her the stubbornness and thirst for adventure. He'd bestowed on her the ability to stand up for what she believed. Even Mother couldn't find fault with the words on the page. Maybe someday Annie would know why her mother struggled so hard to turn her into her version of a lady.

She turned and caught a glimpse of her mother, hat firmly in place on her head, striding toward the church in the distance. Annie had hurt her feelings by requesting to stay home, but being constantly surrounded by people every day made her crave a few moments of solitude.

The sun rose above the horizon, illuminating the canyon walls, revealing their stripes of mauve and rose. Did they look the same from below or was the view from above a special one? She'd promised herself she would go on the next tour Dallas led, but her work schedule hadn't allowed the time yet. The latest group was due back late that afternoon. One of the guests was a pastor who thought it would be a good idea to have a small church service at the river's edge. How glorious that must be.

Annie had begged for permission to go, but her mother had denied it, again, and Dallas had turned and left the room without supporting her. Annie sighed. What could he do? He wasn't family; he was only an employee. As long as Annie lived at home, Mother's word was, and always would be, law.

Sometimes Annie wished she'd been born male, but then she would read something in God's word, like the scripture she'd read that morning, and repent of her ungrateful thinking.

A hawk soared and screeched, dancing on the same breeze that kissed Annie's cheeks. She closed her eyes and lifted her face heavenward. The chance to be outside was the greatest gift she could have. She turned and eyed the hotel. Maybe she could convince them to install an outdoor dining room. Would that be something customers would appreciate?

Annie shrugged. Probably not. It was a silly idea. Most of the dining guests were pressed for time and didn't have the luxury of enjoying a leisurely meal. If folks wanted to sit outside, they occupied one of the many rockers on the expansive front porch.

That could be another perk of the boardinghouse! They could offer picnic lunches beside the canyon rim for those lacking the courage to venture to the canyon floor. Of course, most of the perks would have to be free of charge, since the idea behind them was to entice folks to stay at the more modest accommodations, but there was little difference between eating at a table or on a beautiful quilt, right?

She sighed with the romance of the idea of sharing a meal on the canyon rim with a handsome man. At the age of nineteen, she wondered whether a man would ever look at her like she hung the moon. She bent her knees and wrapped her arms around them, resting her chin on top. Maybe if she weren't so outspoken... At least that was Mother's explanation for why Annie had no suitors.

But then again, it had been a long time since she'd thought twice about a man...until Dallas Baker arrived on their doorstep.

"Annie?" Mother peered down at her. "Why are you sleeping on the ground? Are you ill?"

"I must have dozed off." She sat up and tried to straighten her hair.

"There are people standing on the porch." Mother put her hands on her hips. "They are looking for their room assignments. Gracious, girl. When I heard that and couldn't find you...well, never mind. Come help me."

Annie's face flamed. She smoothed her skirt and

followed her mother back to the house. A young couple and a middle-aged man smiled with amusement at her. She ducked her head and hurried inside.

But, oh, the nap had felt wonderful! Late nights conversing with Dallas on the porch and long days behind the lunch counter at El Tovar added up to exhaustion. Maybe a Sunday nap should become a regular occurrence.

"Welcome." Mother smiled and removed her hat. "Forgive us. We take Sunday mornings off to attend church." She cut a sideways glance at Annie. "My daughter will assign your rooms." With a curt nod, she moved into the dining room.

Annie handed the guests their room keys. "Breakfast is served at 7:00 a.m. Lunch and dinner may be purchased with at least an hour's notice. Otherwise, the El Tovar serves excellent meals. With a dress code, of course." She handed each of the guests a pamphlet listing the rules and amenities. With a smile at the younger couple, she added,. "And we offer picnics beside the canyon. Just let my mother know if you'd like that option."

They beamed at each other and the young man grabbed the girl's hand. "That sounds lovely. We're on our honeymoon."

Annie had guessed as much. "Congratulations. I hope you enjoy your stay in Williams."

Once the guests had headed up the stairs, Annie went to inform her mother of the latest perk the B and B was now offering.

Mother sighed and turned, leaning her back against the counter. "Do you realize that all your newfangled ideas create more work, rather than lessening my load?"

"I'm sorry." Annie took a step back. "I thought I was helping to assure you of a good livelihood."

"I will definitely have to hire help. With the baking, cleaning, cooking meals on demand, why, I don't know which end is up half the time." She pulled a pan and wooden spoon from a shelf.

"I could quit working at the hotel and help you."

Mother waved the spoon at her. "Definitely not! That is our best option for finding you a husband."

*

Rascal's head cleared the rim of the canyon. Dallas guided the horse next to where the tour guests dismounted in front of the barn. "Having a church service in the canyon was an excellent idea, Pastor."

The man nodded. "I find myself closer to God outside than between the walls of a building."

"I very much agree." Annie approached, clapping. "I spent this morning outside with God's word myself."

The pastor, Sean McMurray, turned to greet her. His eyes widened and his face lit up. "Miss Rollins, I shouldn't be surprised." He handed his mule's reins to Dallas. "I'd be pleased if you'd join me next week for my outdoor devotions."

"I'd love to, Pastor McMurray." She accepted his offered arm, and he led her into the house.

Dallas stifled a growl. Why should he feel jealous that Annie and McMurray hit it off? The two were well suited for each other. The man seemed appreciative of Annie's uniqueness.

Gathering all the reins together, Dallas led the mules inside the barn. His stomach rumbled, but he'd need to take care of the animals first. Had Annie invited McMurray to stay for supper? He was a guest at El

Tovar, but it would be just like the kind-hearted girl to ask him.

Dallas needed to hurry. If the two were going to form a friendship, then Dallas needed to make sure the man had Annie's best interests at heart. His hands stilled. Of course McMurray did. He was a man of God. Dallas shook his head, trying to rid himself of his jealous feelings.

He valued Annie's friendship. That's why the thought of the other man unnerved him. Dallas was afraid Annie's attentions would be focused somewhere else. Sure, that was it. What a fool he was being.

Finished with the evening chores, he washed his face and arms at the outdoor pump before entering the kitchen through the back door.

Mrs. Rollins turned with a smile. "Just in time for supper. Do you mind carrying in the roast?"

"Not at all." Dallas lifted the platter, carried it into the dining room and set it in the center of the table. As he'd assumed, McMurray was sitting next to Annie. An older man occupied the chair next to where Mrs. Rollins usually sat. Dallas had thought regular meals were no longer provided for guests. He chose the seat across from Annie.

"Dallas, this is Mr. Harris. He's a guest here," Annie said. "You know Mr. McMurray. We have some newlyweds staying also, but they are dining at the El Tovar."

Dallas nodded a greeting to Mr. Harris. When the man's grin widened upon the appearance of Mrs. Rollins, Dallas suspected the reason the gentleman was staying for supper. He hid a grin of his own. It would be good for the widow to find another husband. Maybe then she'd give Annie the freedom to be who she wanted to be.

"I'm thinking of possibly canceling my stay at the El Tovar," McMurray said, his gaze never leaving Annie's face. "But knowing you are one of the beautiful waitresses there stills my hand."

She pressed her lips together and reached for the bowl of roasted potatoes. "That shouldn't matter, Mr. McMurray. I'm sure we'll see plenty of each other."

Dallas concentrated on buttering his roll so the others wouldn't see the smile on his face. So, McMurray was seeking a bride and Annie was less than thrilled. Dallas's heart lifted. Selfish thought or not, he wouldn't be losing his friend anytime soon.

"I'm counting on it." McMurray spread his napkin in his lap. "Why, I caught a glimpse of heaven when I walked through those doors."

Annie rolled her eyes.

Mrs. Rollins sat up straighter. "Have another slice of roast, Mr. McMurray."

Dallas chuckled, eliciting a kick under the table from Annie.

"This part of Arizona is chock-full of beautiful ladies." Mr. Harris nodded at Mrs. Rollins.

Her cheeks turned pink. "What a nice thing to say." She served him a heaping spoonful of green beans.

Annie glanced from her mother to the man, then at Dallas. Her eyebrows rose. He shrugged. He had no idea what was going on, but it seemed suspiciously like a matchmaking service. A gentleman for each of the Rollins women. Dallas wanted no part of it. He rushed through his meal, declining dessert.

"Thank you for the supper. Delicious as always." He

scooted back his chair and stood.

"I'll walk you to the door." Annie hurried to his side.

"All right." Dallas frowned. She'd never escorted him out before. Once they were out of the others' hearing, he took her by the elbow. "What's going on?"

"Don't leave me back there. Can't you see what my mother is doing?" Annie pulled her arm free.

Dallas led her to the porch. "She's encouraging the attention of an eligible man."

"She's trying to marry me off!" Annie plopped into a rocker. "And she seems to have the same plan for herself."

"I noticed." He sat in the chair next to her. "Would that be so wrong? Someday, you'll find a husband and she'll be alone."

"I'm not talking about her." Annie cupped her head in her palms. "I've told her countless times I'm not looking for a husband. At least not yet. With my job as a Harvey waitress, and helping her run the boardinghouse, there's little time for courting. Not to mention that I still intend to explore the canyon." She shook her head. "No, I have too many plans that marriage would only hinder."

"Unless you were to find the right husband. Someone with the same outlook on life as you have."

"All the men I've met want to turn me into someone I'm not. Even you have old-fashioned ideas about women." She leaped to her feet and ran inside, leaving Dallas speechless.

8

Annie glanced up from wiping down the lunch counter and grinned at the sight of Dallas entering the hotel dining room. His hair, slicked back from a recent dousing, brushed the collar of the borrowed suit jacket he wore. Maybe she could offer to give him a haircut. Her fingers tightened around the rag. Would his hair feel as soft as it looked?

"Close your mouth and stop staring." Dottie glared. "I've had my eye on that man for quite a while now, and I'll not be stepping aside so you can have him." She patted her auburn pompadour. One side was poufed higher than the other. Annie scrubbed the counter harder to prevent herself from smiling at the other girl's obvious attempt at copying her hairstyle.

Other than the Harvey Girls, women were few and far between in this part of the country. Pa had always thought the times would change and families would flock to the area in droves. Well, Annie was still waiting. So was Mother, obviously. Families meant more respectable men to parade in front of Annie as prospective husband material.

"Good morning, ladies." Dallas sat in Annie's section.

Dottie grinned and grabbed the coffeepot, ignoring her customers. "It's so good to see you, Mr. Baker. Your friendly face brightens up the place."

"Thank you, Miss…?"

"Flannery. But you can call me Dottie." She poured him a mug of coffee, flashed him another smile, then moved down the counter.

Annie chuckled. "Careful, or that girl will have a ring on your finger. She emphatically told me she's got her eye on you."

"Did she have a reason for telling you that?" His eyes twinkled as he sipped his hot drink.

"What reason would she have?" The nerve of the man. Annie didn't have her eye on anyone, much less the man who'd stolen her dream. "Why would I jeopardize our friendship for a young girl's jealousy?"

"Why would she be jealous?" Dallas leaned his elbows on the counter and lowered his voice. "Were you two talking about me?"

Oh, she wanted to dump a pitcher of water over his head. Why must he tease her so? He knew as well as anyone she didn't want to get married anytime soon. Then why did her blood rush when he walked into the room? Why did her eyes search for him when he returned from a guide trip?

Having him around threatened all her plans, ones she'd set in place long before he arrived. Between

Dallas and her mother, Annie didn't know which way was up. She tossed the washrag under the counter. "Are you going to order anything? If not, I've other customers."

His eyes clouded over. "Did I say something wrong? If you don't want me here, I can scoot down easy enough."

"Of course I don't want you to move, but I'm sure Dottie wouldn't mind. If you're in the market for a bride, you might look there."

He glanced in the other girl's direction. "She's pretty enough. Mighty young, though."

"Only a year younger than me."

He shrugged. "You act older."

What did he mean by that? Annie pulled her bottom lip between her teeth. Did he think her an old maid? That she didn't know how to have fun? She'd show him the next time he took a group down to the canyon floor. Allowed to or not, she'd accompany him.

"Go sit somewhere else." Annie set her chin and moved to the next customer, plastering on a smile.

"Fine." Dallas set his mug down with a clunk, tossed his borrowed jacket on his stool and stormed from the restaurant.

Annie blinked back tears, knowing she had acted like a child, but not knowing how to fix the situation. Mother told her constantly she was in danger of being a spinster. Annie didn't want a handsome man, one whose opinion she valued, to agree with her mother.

"What did you say to make him leave so quickly?" Dottie stared at the door. "He prettied the place up."

"Don't be silly." Annie slid past her to fetch a fresh pot of coffee. "El Tovar is one of the best hotels in the

Harvey chain. The place is beautiful."

"You know what I mean."

The train whistle blew and the customers moved as one for the door. Annie let her smile fade. Her shoulders slumped. She should count herself lucky and heed the words she gave Dottie.

El Tovar was beautiful with its log-style front desk and wood floors. It was the most modern place she'd ever stepped foot in. Why, the hotel had its own greenhouse and chickens! Hot and cold running water, indoor plumbing, its own barbershop, an art gallery.

Yes, she worked in a beautiful place, so why didn't she enjoy her job more? It wasn't the hard work. She was used to that. The girls were friendly enough, although several had broken their contracts to get married since Annie had joined the company. The waitresses were a revolving circle of faces.

She grabbed a broom and started sweeping behind the counter, then stopped and leaned on the broom handle. She hadn't learned to be content with what she had or where she was. Hadn't the apostle Paul said something about that very subject in Philippians? Annie wouldn't be happy wherever she was planted unless she learned to be content in her present circumstances first. She stared out the window.

And...she owed Dallas an apology.

*

Dallas slapped his hat against his thigh and marched down the steps of the hotel. Having nothing pressing to work his hand at, he had too much time to stew over Annie's attitude. The woman had been downright shrewish. Not like her at all. More like the Annie he'd first met.

He arrived back at the boardinghouse within minutes and ran an experienced eye over the property. Pine needles blanketed the ground, the porch needed a coat of paint and one of the shingles hung askew. There was plenty of work that needed to be done. If Mrs. Rollins didn't mind, he could putter at it in between his guide trips, especially with Horace disappearing on a regular basis. If Dallas remembered correctly, there was a toolbox in the barn.

"I'm sorry."

He turned to see Annie standing under the pine trees, hands twisting her apron. If she didn't stop, the head waitress was sure to give her a demerit for wrinkles.

"I'm out of sorts today and took it out on you. That was inexcusable." Her chin quivered, sending his heart to his toes.

Adventurous Annie with tears in her eyes? That wouldn't do at all. "Apology accepted. I shouldn't have teased you." He chucked her under the chin. "Still friends?"

She knocked his hand away. "Don't treat me like a child, Dallas."

"My turn to apologize." He scratched his head and continued heading toward the barn. Something had Annie riled, and he was at a total loss as to how to set things right.

"What are you doing?" She trotted along beside him.

"Shouldn't you be at work?" He slid aside the board that held the doors closed and pushed them open.

"We're on a break. I've only got a minute."

He found the toolbox in the corner. "I thought I'd work on some of the repairs around here. I'm not one to stay idle, and there aren't any tours scheduled for the next few days."

"Mother can't afford to pay you." Annie stood in the doorway, the sunlight catching her hair, giving her a golden halo.

"I'm not asking to be paid."

"Oh." She scuffed her shoe in the dirt and sighed. "I've been resentful toward you because you can freely go where I want to and can't." The words came out rushed, as if she'd forced them between clenched teeth. "My resentment is hurtful and uncalled for, but it's the way I feel. Again, I apologize, and don't want to lose our friendship." With a swish of her skirt, she was gone.

Women were the most confusing things. Dallas hefted the heavy box and moved to the porch. Annie, in her black-and-white uniform, flew toward the restaurant like an exotic bird.

He felt for her, wanting to go to the canyon floor and not being allowed to. Maybe he could convince Mrs. Rollins to go on a camping trip, too, thus allowing Annie to experience her dream.

He set the tools on the floor and dug inside the box for a hammer and nails. Finding them, he wiggled the loose shutter into place and nailed it securely.

After he'd fixed the third shutter, Mrs. Rollins stepped onto the porch. "What is all the racket?"

Dallas removed the nails he held between his teeth. "I'm making some necessary repairs, Mrs. Rollins. I hope you don't mind."

"I like a man who doesn't relish being idle, but I can't afford to pay you anything extra."

"Annie said as much. I'm not looking for more money. The room and board, plus what you pay for the tours, is plenty." He wasn't raised to sit around and be a man of leisure. When the work was slow, he spent too much time at the hotel nursing cups of coffee. Obviously, his presence there bothered Annie. He'd have to cut back on his visits.

"Maybe I could get you to deliver my baked goods each morning? Often there's too much for Annie to carry by herself."

"Annie's idea is working for you, is it?" Why was his employer talkative all of a sudden? Rare were the times he actually carried on a conversation with her.

"My girl definitely has a head for business. Too bad that won't do her much good in this world. She needs to settle down and run a household. Lucky is the man who corners her." With a nod, Mrs. Rollins went back in the house.

The only part of the conversation Dallas didn't agree with was that Annie's business sense was a waste in a woman. Why, his mother kept the accounts for the ranch. She looked like a lady and thought like a man, when the need arose. That was the type of woman Dallas wanted to marry. Annie was making strides toward being the perfect model for a wife, except for the fact that she wore her split skirt at every opportunity. She was pretty as a sunset, had a good head on her shoulders, and strong morals. Mrs. Rollins was right. Annie would make some man a good wife.

With the shingles in place, Dallas went in search of a rake. Once he'd found it, he set to work raking up the pine needles. With the wind down, it was a perfect day to burn off the dead leaves and grass. They didn't have many windless days on the canyon's rim.

His stomach rumbled, reminding him supper was near. Which also meant Annie would be home soon.

Mrs. Rollins served the meal late so Annie wouldn't have to eat alone. The proprietress might seem crusty, but Dallas suspected a soft heart resided under her starched aprons. A heart that loved her daughter very much.

He spotted someone wearing the familiar Harvey uniform. Setting the rake aside, he prepared himself to meet her, hoping Annie's mood had improved. As the woman neared, he realized it wasn't Annie at all, but Dottie.

With a large grin on her face.

9

Annie dumped her armload of dirty napkins into a laundry bin. "I'm heading home, Miss Cartwright, if that's all right with you. Mother always holds supper until I get home."

"That's fine." The head waitress sighed and stared out the back window of the kitchen. "Maybe the Harvey Company should hire ugly girls. I've lost two more to marriage this week." She turned and patted Annie on the shoulder. "Thank you, girl, for your faithfulness. I know working here wasn't your choice, but at least I know I can count on you."

Annie stood in stunned silence as the woman left the room. Did Miss Cartwright believe her to be unmarriageable? Mother had hopes that Annie *would* find a husband by working at El Tovar. Was it possible that no man wanted her for a wife? Could it be that Mother had found her the job so she'd have a means of supporting herself as a spinster? Annie clutched the fabric of her neckline.

"Your mother's pastries are very popular," Mr. Swanson, the chef, said as he entered the room from the pantry. "Serving them at the lunch counter for breakfast was a great idea. You've a good head on your shoulders."

"Thank you." Annie almost asked the man whether he thought her pretty, but bit back the words. It wouldn't be proper. Folks were always saying how smart she was, how stubborn, but no one ever said whether she was pretty.

She shouldn't worry so much that a man might propose. Chances were…one wouldn't. She'd had herself in turmoil since her first day at the hotel for absolutely no reason. She banged through the back door and stepped onto the lawn.

Stars dotted the sky. Gas lamps strategically placed along a path broke the darkness. Annie didn't stop to enjoy any of the beauty. She had thrown a lovely young woman at the only man who seemed interested in keeping company with her, and now she had accepted the fact that she wasn't prime marriage material.

What would she do for the rest of her life? Be a head waitress like Miss Cartwright? Take over the business from Mother or run it as her partner? Annie's eyes stung. None of those options was what she'd imagined for her future. Foolish girl that she was, she'd actually thought that someday, after enjoying a bit of freedom, she'd find a man to marry and have a family with. Someone like Dallas. But now, with Annie on the verge of spinsterhood, at least in everyone else's eyes, her choices were limited.

She tossed Dallas a wave as he stared down at Dottie's petite frame under a massive pine, not really caring whether he saw her or not. Why should she care? She'd sent the girl to his side, after all, in a foolish attempt to mend her friendship with the only man that interested her.

Pushing the screen door of the B and B open, she took care not to let it slam behind her. She stood and listened for Mother's words of welcome instead of condemnation. Nothing but silence greeted her. No smells of supper cooking or pastry orders baking, not even the odor of the pungent vinegar her mother used in cleaning. "Mother?"

Annie's footsteps sounded abnormally loud on the wood floors. The only boarder left was the widower Mr. Harris, so it was quite possible he had retired to his room, but Mother's absence worried Annie. It wasn't like her not to be in the kitchen or working on the books at this time of the early evening.

A bowl of stew and a slice of cornbread waited for her in the warming oven. Maybe Mother had gone to her room with a headache. It wasn't a frequent occurrence, but wasn't unheard of. Waking her when she nursed a headache was like waking a sleeping bear. If Annie didn't see her within a few minutes, she'd risk checking on her. She took her supper to the back porch and sat at one of the small tables.

Since Mother was nowhere around to tell her the action was unladylike, Annie crumbled her bread into her stew. She could act like a lady if she wanted to. After all, she did so all day at the hotel. At home, she wanted to be herself. There was no one watching but God, and since she wasn't doing anything evil or against His Word, she felt secure in the fact that He wouldn't condemn her.

What did her heavenly Father want her to do? Remain a single businesswoman or marry? Maybe if Annie actually put her mind to hunting for a husband, she'd find one that didn't mind her tall lankiness and outspoken manner. She considered her prospects.

Other than the endless men who came through on the trains, there were only Dallas and Pastor McMurray, who for some reason unknown to her was still in town. The town wasn't large enough for two preachers, and Pastor Carson managed fine without help other than his dear wife, Sophie.

Her eyes widened. Was it possible that Pastor McMurray was staying around because of here? He was good-looking enough to garner her attention, but a bit boring to converse with, if she was honest. Other than the fact he seemed to love the canyon as much as she did, and obviously had a strong faith in God, the man had nothing else in common with her. Were those two things enough for a happy marriage?

Then there was Dallas. Except for his stupid ideas about what made a perfect wife, he had all the qualities Annie admired. Handsome, smart, adventurous, a good conversationalist. She scooped a spoonful of stew. Why, he'd make the perfect husband if she could change his way of thinking.

Voices drew her from her thoughts and she peered through the growing darkness. A man and woman, hand in hand, strolled from a thick stand of trees on a well-worn path that curved for quite a distance along the canyon's edge.

Annie dropped her spoon. "Mother?"

*

Dallas went around the corner of the house as Mrs. Rollins and Mr. Harris came out of the trees. Dallas turned at Annie's exclamation, not having noticed her on the porch. Her mouth hung open and stew dotted her white apron.

"Good evening, Annie, Dallas." Mrs. Rollins pulled her hand free from Mr. Harris's. "Lovely night, isn't it?" She put a foot on the bottom step. "Good. I see my daughter found her supper. It appears she's wearing some of it."

Annie grabbed a napkin from beside her bowl and scrubbed at the bodice of her apron. "Don't just stand there, Dallas, do something," she said after her mother and Mr. Harris entered the house.

"What would you like me to do? I can't rub off the stew. It wouldn't be proper." He supposed he could carry her dishes inside.

Her eyes widened, shining from the reflection of the nearby gas lantern. "Not my apron! My mother. If she's going to be keeping company with a man we hardly know, don't you think it wise that someone question him as to his intentions?"

"Why me?" He leaned against the railing and watched a moth flutter around the lamp. The bug got too close, and a faint hiss issued as its wing came into contact with the hot glass.

"With Pa dead, you're the likely candidate." Annie gathered her dishes and waited for him to open the door for her.

Strange. Usually, she'd have shouldered her way through without his help. He opened the door. "I'm only an employee, Annie. Not part of the family."

"Fine." She tilted her chin. "I'll do it myself, although it might be better if the questions came from a man."

Dallas closed the door and scratched his head. Who was this girl, and what had she done with his Annie? "No, if it means that much, I'd be happy to take over. I'll talk to him at the first opportunity."

"Tonight."

"Excuse me?"

She turned with a flutter of her eyelashes and a pretty pout. "I need it settled right away, please."

Mesmerized by the new version of Annie, Dallas nodded. "I'll look for him right now." He headed toward the parlor. In the evening, the man either spent time there reading or on the porch enjoying a cigar. After checking the house, Dallas found him on the porch. They must have circled each other during Dallas's search.

"Mr. Harris, mind if I join you?"

"Not at all. Would you care for a smoke?" He offered a cigar from a tin box.

"No, thank you." How in the world did one question a stranger as to his intentions? Especially when the lady in question was not a relative?

Dallas lowered himself into the rocker next to Mr. Harris.

"Something on your mind, son?" Mr. Harris blew a smoke ring. A soft breeze caught it, warping its shape as it dissipated.

"Yes, sir." Dallas took a deep breath. "Miss Rollins has asked me to find out what your intentions are toward her mother."

"Did she now?" He blew a steady stream of smoke.

"Well, you tell that little lady that I intend to marry her mother."

"Pardon my boldness, but why?" Dallas leaned his elbows on his knees and peered into the other man's face. "You hardly know her."

"Sometimes the heart just knows." Mr. Harris ground out his cigar on the bottom of his shoe. "I know Esther can be a bit prickly and a lot bossy, but I love her despite those characteristics. No one is perfect, son. If you wait for the perfect woman, you'll die lonely. We're two middle-aged people not looking forward to spending our older years alone.

"I like the area here, and I can be a great asset to her business, if we don't turn it over to her daughter to run. We've considered traveling the Santa Fe Railroad to see this great country of ours." He stood and clapped Dallas on the shoulder. "It's good of you to worry about these fine women, but rest assured, my intentions are honorable." He left Dallas alone.

That went well. Dallas set the rocker in motion, knowing Annie would soon join him. He wasn't disappointed. The door had barely shut behind Mr. Harris before she rushed out.

"Tell me." She took the chair vacated by her mother's suitor. "Does he plan to marry her?"

"Yes."

Annie sat so long without speaking, Dallas would have thought she'd gone inside except that he could smell the rose-scented soap she'd washed with. Instead of her uniform, she now wore the dreaded split skirt with a flowered blouse. He shook his head, wishing she'd worn a regular, feminine skirt. He didn't mind the puffy hairdo. It led him to believe that, brushed out, the strands would fall down her back like a golden waterfall. His fingers itched to feel her hair's softness. He sat on his hand rather than embarrass himself. "Are you upset that your mother may be married soon?"

"I'm not sure." She started rocking, a rhythmic squeak joining the conversation. "I shouldn't be. After all, I want my mother to be happy, but it seems so sudden."

He nodded. "I guess things move faster as people get older."

"Maybe. Did you enjoy Dottie's company?"

He turned to stare at her. "Did you send her?"

She shrugged. "She likes you. A lot."

"That was the first time I'd spoken more than a few words to the girl, and she's as immature as I feared." Dottie had asked him whether he liked her new hairstyle and whether the Harvey uniform drowned out her complexion. He felt certain he'd lost some of his intelligence by carrying on the simple conversation. "I don't need help finding a girl, Annie."

"All right." She stood. "Thank you for your help tonight. I felt questioning the man should be left to a man. You did admirably."

There she went again, being all sweet and defenseless. Did all women have two such contrasting sides? He directed his thoughts to his mother. No, Ma seemed the same all the time.

What in the world had gotten into Annie?

10

Another Sunday, and Annie had agreed to spend the afternoon with Pastor McMurray. She made a face at her reflection in the mirror. While no one else had made any references during the past week in regards to her impending spinsterhood, Annie decided it was time to take steps to prevent becoming the subject of people's pity. So, since Dallas was out of the question with his old-fashioned ideas about wives, she chose another man who loved the Grand Canyon.

After sticking the last pin into her hair, she smoothed her split skirt and straightened the collar on her blue blouse. The color brightened her eyes. With pinches to her cheeks, she headed downstairs to the kitchen, where Mother had made a picnic basket.

"He's waiting in the parlor." Mother handed her the basket. "You took too long." She eyed Annie's skirt and sighed. "Really, daughter, I thought you could at least wear a proper dress or skirt today. Do you want to run him off before he's even had a chance to get to know you?"

"I don't want a man if he doesn't want me the way I am." Annie snatched the basket from her hands and marched to the parlor, where a folded quilt lay on one of the chairs.

Pastor McMurray turned from studying a photograph on the fireplace mantel. "Your father?"

"Yes." Tears stung Annie's eyes. "We miss him."

"You have his bearing. Please, allow me to carry that." He took the basket from her and crooked his free arm.

Annie grabbed the quilt and grasped his elbow. What did he mean, "Papa's bearing"? Did that mean she was stout? Manly? Annie wasn't sure she liked Pastor McMurray at all. Even the roughest of men rarely commented on a woman's form, especially in a derogatory way. She clamped her lips shut before she said something she shouldn't.

She caught Mother peeking around the corner of the kitchen door and waved her away. If the grin on her face was any indication, she was already planning Annie's wedding.

She allowed the pastor to lead her outside, then headed away from her favorite overlook. That was a special place. One he hadn't earned the right to enjoy with her yet. Instead, she motioned for him to go farther down the canyon's edge until they reached a cleared area under some pine trees.

"Will this do, Pastor?" she asked. At his nod, she spread out the blanket.

"Please call me Sean. I don't have a church here and

would like to think you call me friend." He set the basket on a corner of the quilt, then lay on his side, crooking his arm and resting his head in his hand. "What a beautiful day for a picnic. You're lucky to live here."

"Mostly. Winters can be harsh." She lowered herself to the blanket, sitting with her legs to the side and wondering why she didn't feel like indulging in conversation. The man was pleasant enough, even good-looking in a slimmer, not as tough as Dallas sort of way.

She studied him from lowered lashes as she set out the food. Auburn hair was slicked back from a face with sharp angles and eyes the shade of pine needles that had plenty of rain. Although he'd carried the basket, he now lay there as if he were a king waiting to be waited on. Annie had no idea what to talk about. Hopefully, Sean would carry the conversation.

He accepted a glass of lemonade she offered him. "Do you enjoy your job at the El Tovar?"

"It's wonderful as far as jobs go." She sipped her drink, trying not to grimace at the sweetness. She preferred her lemonade a little more tart. "Most of the girls are friendly and the head waitress is easy to work for."

"It must be wonderful training for a woman to learn the proper ways of running a home." He smiled. "Not that most young ladies don't learn at their mother's knee, but with the company's strict rules, it reinforces what has already been learned, correct?"

Annie tried not to roll her eyes. Did every man in northern Arizona have antiquated ideas? "Do you believe that ladies can't have opinions of their own?"

"Why, certainly they can." Sean straightened. "They just shouldn't express them in here, and definitely not in mixed company." He reached across the space between them and set his hand on hers. "I can see that you are a beautiful, yet willful woman. You may feel free to express your opinions when we are alone. I promise to give them my utmost consideration."

"Why, that is mighty kind of you." She slipped her hand free and tossed him a sandwich. What she wanted to do was throw it against his head.

"I do try to take people's feelings into consideration." He picked up the sandwich and smiled again.

How soon could Annie plead a headache and get this picnic over with? She stifled a sigh. Mother would kill her if she didn't at least make an honest attempt toward getting to know Sean. She forced a smile in return. "That is very Christian of you."

"That's a good thing for a man in my position."

Yes, he definitely seemed to enjoy his own company very much. Annie glanced toward the canyon. There was a safe topic to discuss. "Tell me about your trip to the canyon floor."

"One of God's greatest creations."

Annie hung on his every word as he described the plants and animals he'd seen, the brisk-running river, the eagles flying overhead. She could tell from the contented look on Sean's face that he assumed a different meaning from her rapt interest than she intended, but he had been where she so desired to go.

She could barely eat her sandwich as he described how the striped walls of the canyon looked as if they were painted by God's paintbrush and how darkness fell so much quicker as the walls blocked out the sun.

While they'd held their simple church service, a hawk had soared on a current of air, lending its cries to their worship. Tears filled Annie's eyes, and she put a hand to her chest at how beautiful it all sounded.

A shadow fell across the blanket.

*

Why was Annie crying? Pastor or not, if McMurray did or said anything to upset her, Dallas would knock him flat. "What's going on here?"

Annie smiled through her tears. "Sean was describing his trip to the canyon floor. It sounds beautiful."

Sean? They were on a first-name basis? Dallas's heart fell to his knees. Maybe he really was nothing more than an employee. Most likely, thinking he and Annie were friends was all in his mind. He turned to leave.

"Would you like to join us?" Annie patted the quilt. "Mother packed plenty of food."

Dallas noticed the scowl on Sean's face. "No, thanks. I've work to do."

"On a Sunday?" Annie frowned.

"The, uh, animals still need tending." He hurried away before she asked more questions. The animals didn't need feeding for hours, and Annie would know that if she thought about it for a moment. He'd embarrass himself if she called him back.

Mrs. Rollins didn't serve meals on Sunday except for breakfast. Most times, she invited him to dine with them anyway, since he was the only hired hand. Today, he needed a pretty face and conversation. He headed for El Tovar.

Dottie was working the lunch counter with a girl Dallas didn't know. Without thinking too hard on it, he picked a stool in Dottie's section. If he'd stopped to consider, he might have realized how the gesture would encourage her. Wrong or not, Dallas needed a gal to pay him some attention.

"Mr. Baker!" Dottie's faint brogue rolled off her tongue. "Coffee?"

"Please." He studied the menu and chose a bowl of chicken soup. The hotel served huge chunks of fresh bread with their soup. Exactly what his stomach needed.

Dottie poured his coffee and leaned one hip against the counter. "I'm usually off on Sundays, but one of the other girls took sick. Maybe we could sit next to each other at church next Sunday."

"Maybe." Dallas flashed her a grin. She really was a cute little thing, if a bit immature. Maybe that could actually work in her favor. A man could teach her the things she needed to know in order to keep him happy.

Something his ma said once niggled at his brain. Something about a woman being a man's helpmate, not his maid. He brushed the thought aside. He must remember it wrong. Ma always waited on Pa hand and foot. She seemed to enjoy her role as wife and mother. That's what Dallas wanted. A gal just like his ma.

He turned on his stool when Dottie moved to serve another customer, and studied the girls flitting around the room. Every one of them was comely. They all had a smile that led each customer to feel as if he or she were the only person in the place.

Annie could do that, too. Even while showing how much spirit she had. Dallas grinned. Annie would take some taming. Too bad he wouldn't be the one to do so. No, a ranch took a lot of work. It didn't leave time to teach a woman how to do things.

Turning back around, he lifted his mug. Maybe a spirited wife wouldn't be a bad thing. Annie was fun and spoke of current events with intelligence. Could Dallas possibly be wrong in the traits he was looking for in a woman?

He continued to watch Dottie and the other girls. What were they like when not in uniform? It was quite possible he couldn't judge a woman by the job she did at the hotel. "Dottie, I'd like to take a walk with you after work tonight, if you're willing."

"Oh, Mr. Baker, I'd be most pleased. Or, if you'd rather, we have a parlor upstairs where we can entertain company."

That might be best. He'd heard of the strict moral rules for the girls. It could also be less intimate with a chaperone. He didn't want to lead Dottie on falsely, just get to know how different the girls were when out of their stiff dark dresses.

He'd noticed how several of them were wearing their hair in the same high upsweep as Annie. Hopefully, Dottie wouldn't arrive in the parlor with a split skirt. If so, Dallas would have lost all hope in women.

"Thanks for the coffee, Dottie. I'll be around after supper." He nodded and headed back outside. He was relieved to see that Annie and McMurray no longer stared into each other's eyes under the pine trees. He didn't think he could stomach any more of their courting that day.

He spotted Annie sitting on her familiar log, and considered going on into the barn without stopping. But the sun glinting on her golden hair, and the breeze teasing the few fair strands that had come loose, drew him.

"Mind if I sit a spell?" he asked, turning his hat around his hands. When had he become shy around her?

"Certainly." She scooted over and moved her skirt aside.

"How was your picnic?"

She shrugged. "Confusing."

He hoped she'd elaborate. When she didn't, he asked, "How so?"

"The only thing Sean and I seem to have in common is our love of the canyon. He has the same old-fashioned ideas as—" she glared at him "—most of the men around these parts."

Dallas couldn't help the leap of joy in his heart that her picnic had been less than perfect. "Surely the man has something that drew you to spend time with him."

"Well…" She scrunched up her nose and gazed into the distance. "He's fairly handsome and quite intelligent. Not to mention he's a man of God. He'd make someone like my mother the perfect husband."

"What about you?"

She speared him with her glance. "He has definitely not been struck off my list of prospects."

She had a list of potential husbands?

11

Annie placed menus on tables set with fine china and starched white tablecloths. Soon, hotel guests would arrive for breakfast and the first train of the day would pull into the station. The quiet of the morning would erupt with noise. Although she went home each night with exhaustion weighing on her shoulders like a heavy blanket, she didn't mind the work too much. With her salary she was able to help her mother and keep aside a bit for herself. Pa used to say any honest work was often hard. Well, there wasn't a job much more honest than that of a Harvey Girl.

She lifted her head and glanced out the window. Already a few hotel guests rocked on the massive front porch, newspapers or novels in hand. She transferred her attention to the ceiling above. What were the rooms like? What luxuries did the hotel offer? Somehow, she needed to find a way to look around. Then she could come up with new ideas for the boardinghouse. They needed to either modernize or close.

The girls' dorms were on the top floor. What would prevent Annie from "visiting"? Since she went home each evening, would she be allowed to see the parlor? What would happen if she were caught peeking into empty rooms on the guest floor?

"Good morning, Annie." Miss Cartwright bustled past with a basket of rolled silverware. "Do you mind setting these out? The other girls are busy in the kitchen rolling."

"No, ma'am." She preferred being busy to being idle. Lack of work allowed her mind to wander in dangerous directions.

"Something on the roof?" Miss Cartwright glanced up.

"No, ma'am. Just thinking." Annie took the basket. "Actually, I was wondering whether I would be able to tour the hotel. I'm curious as to what all it offers."

"And to scout out the competition, I'd wager." The head waitress smiled. "We'll have to ask Mr. Lawrence. He can be a bit prickly about his girls wandering where they aren't allowed, and since you don't live here...well." She patted Annie on the shoulder. "We'll ask him and see."

Annie had just placed the last rolled silverware beside a plate when the doors opened and the breakfast crowd arrived. She hurried to the lunch counter, wondering when she'd have the opportunity to move up in her position. Maybe the prized spot of drink girl went only to the waitresses living at the hotel.

The drink girls only had to glance at the position of a glass in order to know the customer's beverage of choice. Annie did it all at the lunch counter. Not that she was complaining, but maybe with another position, she wouldn't be as exhausted when she went home, and could help out there more.

She turned with a full pot of coffee, and almost dropped the silver-plated carafe when she saw her mother strolling into the restaurant on Mr. Harris's arm. With a wave in Annie's direction, the glowing woman took a seat at one of the dining tables.

Why wasn't she at home baking? The hotel had recently increased its order of morning pastries. Without help, Mother would never manage to fill the order.

"Cover me, Dottie. Please." Annie set the coffee back on its warmer and weaved through the tables to where her mother sat. "This is a surprise."

"Well, yes." She smiled. "Mr. Harris wanted to treat me for once rather than have me wait on him. Since our last boarders just left, I've the time."

Annie tilted her head. "What aren't you telling me?"

"You might as well, Esther. It won't be a secret for long," Mr. Harris said, spreading his napkin in his lap.

Mother took a deep breath. "Mr. Harris proposed to me last night. I was going to tell you when you arrived home this evening that I've said yes."

Annie's knees weakened. "I'm…happy for you. What does this mean for the boardinghouse?"

"Well." Mother looked at Mr. Harris. "We plan on taking a trip to California for our honeymoon, and were hoping you would take over for us. We won't leave until your contract with the Harvey Company is fulfilled. Your experience here will be invaluable for taking over, and I've hired a young Indian girl to help with the baking. She starts tomorrow."

So many changes happening very quickly. "We'll talk more this evening." Annie forced her smile to remain in place, and returned to the counter. The boardinghouse would soon be hers to run as she saw fit. She glanced again at the ceiling. Seeing all the hotel had to offer had just become a priority.

The next hour raced by. When the last customer left the dining room, Annie sagged against the counter and watched as the tables were quickly cleared and reset for the next crowd. The warmth of the room soothed her. With its wood floor, split log walls and big window at the far end, it blended hominess and luxury seamlessly. She'd have to look at the B and B with new eyes and see what improvements could be made.

Maybe advertising in eastern cities would draw folks to the Grand Canyon. The trick would be getting them to check in at the boardinghouse rather than El Tovar. Maybe Dallas would have an idea or two.

She reached under the counter for a rag and wiped the counter, ridding it of crumbs and drips of coffee. The cleaning service kept the wood to such a high sheen, Annie could almost see her reflection.

Dottie sidled close and sighed, folding her hands under her chin. "Guess who I'm keeping company with this evening?"

Annie's heart constricted. "I'm sure I have no idea."

"Mr. Baker."

*

Dallas slicked back his hair and bent to peer into the small mirror on the wall in his room. He donned his best shirt, tempted to exchange it for one of his everyday ones, but Ma would skin him alive if she found out. He was visiting with a pretty gal, so why wasn't he more excited?

No help for it now. He swallowed a sigh and headed down the stairs and outside. Rethinking the plan to sit with Dottie in the parlor, he decided maybe he could entice her to take a stroll instead. The night carried a slight chill, but was nothing a shawl wouldn't cure. It would be better than an uncomfortable parlor under the watchful eyes of the other girls.

He marched toward the hotel. Annie approached from the other direction with her head down. "You'll run into something that way," he told her.

"Good evening, Dallas." She crossed her arms. "I suppose you're headed to see Dottie."

"Yes." He bent to peer into Annie's face. "Is something wrong?"

She shook her head. "Just tired, and running the day's events through my mind. Mother announced her engagement to Mr. Harris this morning. We'll be discussing my taking over the boardinghouse when my contract at the hotel expires."

"How do you feel about that?" Personally, he didn't see much of a future in it for her.

"I'm not sure. There are a lot of things to be considered." She gave him a shaky smile. "Enjoy your evening."

"Thank you. You, too." He watched her climb the stairs and disappear into the two-story house. She needed a husband to take her away from the failing business. Maybe Sean McMurray would be her salvation.

Dallas shoved his hands in the pockets of his wool pants. For some reason, the thought of Annie and

McMurray together caused his heart to ache. He shook his head. What a fool. Here he was on his way to see one girl while thinking of another.

He glanced over his shoulder. The lace curtains in the boardinghouse parlor fell back into place. Had Annie been watching him? Dare he hope so? He grinned, his steps lighter as he headed to his destination.

Stopping at the front desk, he informed the concierge that he was there to see Miss Flannery, then took a seat in one of the leather chairs to wait. Since the girls resided on the third floor, he suspected it would take her a few minutes to appear. Plus girls tended to gussy themselves up more than guys. He grabbed a newspaper and settled back to watch the people file past in ones and twos.

A young couple, obviously newly married, clung to each other as they headed upstairs. An older couple, the gentleman's hand on the lady's back, strolled toward the front porch. Love was in the air, it seemed, although summer was in full bloom rather than spring. He really hoped Dottie would consent to spend their time together outside.

Twenty minutes later, she glided down the staircase, one hand brushing along the banister. She looked very feminine in a gown of green calico and with her hair up in the new fashion. He couldn't help but wonder how she'd do riding to the bottom of the canyon on the back of a mule.

He stood and offered her his arm. "Care for a stroll outside?"

Her eyes widened. "What about a chaperone?"

"Then how about we rock on the porch?"

"I think that would be okay." Maybe they should

worry about a chaperone with the way she pressed against his arm.

Dallas shifted to loosen her grip, instead placing his hand on the small of her back to guide her outside. He chose two rockers at one end of the porch. "We can count the stars from here."

"Oh, I couldn't imagine counting that high." She simpered up at him and smoothed her dress before sitting.

It promised to be an evening of simple conversation. What did one talk about with a stranger? "Tell me about yourself, Dottie. Has your family been in America long?"

"I was born here. The first in my family. Da is a factory worker back East. Ma takes care of my siblings. There're eight other than me."

"How do you like working for the Harvey Company?"

"I love it. I came here to find a husband. The prospects are plentiful." She tilted her head and gave him a soft smile. "What about your family?"

He told her of his family's ranch in Texas and watched her eyes widen greedily. With every word about his family's success, she moved closer, until she practically hung over the arm of her seat. Dallas may have wished for a feminine woman, but he didn't want one interested only in his family's money. No, either his future wife married him as he was, a trail guide, or not at all.

Annie's face swam to the forefront of his mind. She wouldn't care. There was a gal who took a person at face value. If only... He sighed. No sense in bringing up a subject he couldn't change.

"Have you had many prospects?" he asked Dottie.

"Just one." Her breath brushed his cheek. When had she moved her chair so close?

"Are you chilled? Maybe we should move to the visiting parlor." Where it was safer.

"I'm warm enough. You smell nice."

He wouldn't have used his new shaving cream if he'd known how it would attract the beast in a woman.

Her fingers glided over his face. "Such a smooth shave."

He pulled her hands away from his face. "Why don't you settle back in your rocker and let's enjoy the evening."

"I'm enjoying myself just fine." She giggled. "You're a bit nervous. Most men would meet me more than halfway. Are you shy?"

"Not at all." The problem was her wayward behavior. Did she act this way with all men or just him?

"If not, then how about a kiss?"

12

Annie stood at the bottom of the staircase, one foot on the first step, her left hand on the railing. The busy day had allowed no time for her to ask permission. Most likely it wouldn't matter, since she was employed by the Harvey Company. Then why did her heart beat in her throat and her palms sweat?

With a glance around, and a smile at the concierge, she climbed, doing her best to act as if she belonged there. She stopped at the second floor, where guests stayed. The hall stretched in front of her like a gauntlet. Taking a deep breath, she strolled forward, hoping to find an open door she could peek in.

A maid was cleaning a room halfway down the hall. Annie stood in the doorway, taking in the gold floral wallpaper, and sleigh bed with blankets that complimented it. A bureau stood against one wall with a clear trifold mirror on top. A rocking chair was nestled under a window with white, sheer curtains. Not too different from the boardinghouse, except that the furnishings were new and the electric lights left no corner in shadow.

"May I help you, miss?" The maid glanced up from making the bed.

Annie shook her head and backed away. Turning, she located stairs leading to the third floor. This was where the other girls slept, although the hall sported too many rooms for just them. She found the private dormitory rooms at the end of the hall.

The first door she came to led to a small parlor with tasteful, comfortable furniture that would allow six people to sit and converse in front of a fire. Two girls, out of uniform, were enjoying their time off, one with a book, the other with knitting. Annie smiled and continued on her way. The staff bedrooms looked very similar to the guest rooms. So far, the fancy hotel didn't have a lot more to offer than her mother did.

Except for running hot and cold water and the electric lights. Annie sighed. Not to mention the extra amenities such as barbershop, solarium, rooftop garden, billiard room, and art and music rooms. It was possible they could incorporate some of them, though.

She pressed her back against the wall and lightly banged her head. All those things cost money. More money than she or Mother had. Maybe if she put some really deep thought into it, she could come up with something unique.

Sure, the baking helped. A lot, actually. Could it be possible a boardinghouse was no longer the route they should take to earning a living? Yes, they had rooms to spare, but those could be for a special few. The type of folks who actually wanted the simpler life. Otherwise, they could focus on baking. They could sell not only to the restaurant, but to the public as well. Maybe sell outdoor equipment in addition to scheduling tours of the canyon.

She grinned and pushed away from the wall. With no fear of hard work and an intelligent, creative mind, she'd make a success of Rollins's Bakery and Outdoor Equipment. Now, to get Mother to—"

"What are you doing up here?" Dottie glared, hands on her hips. "I'm telling Miss Cartwright. If you don't live here, you don't belong here."

"I told Miss Cartwright." She just didn't tell Mr. Laurence.

Dottie narrowed her eyes. "Why are you so flushed?" She patted her hair. "I'm the one who's been thoroughly kissed. Why, Mr. Baker took my breath away."

Annie wanted to stomp on the other girl's toes. A lady did not kiss and tell. She shoved aside the fact that Dottie had kissed Annie's best friend. She had no intentions of losing Dallas's friendship because he fell for an Irish imp with loose morals. Oh, what a mess she'd made of things. Why had she encouraged the girl to go ahead with her pursuit of Dallas?

"Spreading around the fact you were kissing without a chaperone isn't very becoming behavior." Annie straightened. "You could lose your job."

"Oh, posh." Dottie sashayed down the hall and stopped in front of a door at the end. She turned a simpering smile Annie's way. "Don't be jealous. *That* isn't becoming, either."

Oh! Annie stomped her foot and rushed down the stairs. Tomorrow, she'd request to be moved from the counter to a table. She didn't want to work beside Dottie for another day. Annie might not be ready to get married, but she didn't want to listen to the other girl's bragging for a minute.

She stormed past the front desk, not slowing until she'd left the hotel. She shouldn't let the other girl bother her. Annie and Dallas could remain friends while he courted someone, right? Unless the other girl forbad it, and Dottie was the type to do so. Annie sighed and slowed her pace even more. For the first time in her life, she didn't know what she wanted. Independence or a husband? A husband other than Dallas, or Dallas?

Silly girl. Dallas had never shown any indication that he thought of her romantically at all. In fact, other than trying to be more feminine, Annie hadn't shown interest in him, either. The one thing she did know was that she wanted to experience life a bit and not be looked at as if spinsterhood was her definite future.

She bent and picked up a rock, chucking it at a tree. A yelp let her know it wasn't a tree. Gracious! She lifted her skirts and dashed toward the fallen man. *Lord, forgive me for my temper.*

Look what she'd done. Injured another because of a silly tantrum. She fell to her knees and peered into the man's face. "Dallas?"

*

"Why'd you hit me?" He sat up, a hand to his forehead. "Did I make you mad about something?"

"I'm so sorry. Let me see." She pulled his hand away. "It's too dark. Come into the house and let me tend to you. Can you walk?"

"Of course I can. You hit me in the head, you didn't shoot me in the foot." He wiped his wet hand on his pants, hoping Mrs. Rollins knew how to wash blood out of wool. "So, are you going to tell me why you were throwing rocks?" He opened the front door and stepped into the foyer.

"Someone made me angry. I thought you were a tree."

"What happened?" Mrs. Rollins rushed toward them. "Hurry. Into the kitchen. You're bleeding all over my floor."

"I ran into a rock." Dallas winked at Annie. No sense in her getting into trouble with her ma. The harm was already done.

"Ran into a—" She shook her head. "Never mind. Annette, fetch me some hot water and the medical kit. Sit right here, Mr. Baker." She pulled out a kitchen chair.

He lowered himself onto it and took the towel Annie handed him. Since she'd called her daughter by the long version of her name, there'd be more questions. Guaranteed.

"I don't think you'll need stitches, but you might want the doctor to look at it in the morning to be sure." Mrs. Rollins dabbed at his wound.

He hissed. Good thing he had no tours for a few days. He was bound to have a headache.

"But it will leave a colorful bruise." She wrapped a bandage around his head. "Annette, fetch the poor man some coffee while he tells me what really happened. Considering my daughter is fighting back tears—" Mrs. Rollins dropped the bloody rag into a basin of water "—I'd say she's had a hand in your injury."

"She has a strong arm." Dallas leaned his head against the back of the chair and tried to concentrate on the conversation rather than the throbbing above his left eye.

"It was an accident." Annie sniffed. "I was angry at one of the other girls and threw a rock at what I thought was a tree."

"Of course you did." Mrs. Rollins stood and picked up the basin. "What could possibly make you mad enough to throw rocks?" When Annie didn't answer, she asked the question again.

Annie expelled a hard breath and stabbed Dallas with her glare. "She's going around bragging to everyone about how she managed to get alone with Dallas without proper chaperonage, and how his kisses left her breathless."

Mrs. Rollins stared at her daughter, her mouth slightly open. She bit her bottom lip and went out the back door to dump the water.

Dallas couldn't tear his gaze away from Annie's. Dottie was bragging? It made Annie mad enough to throw rocks? What had he gotten himself into? If he'd known Dottie was prone to flapping her lips, he never would've spent time in her company. It was his fault, after all. He was the one who'd wanted to enjoy the evening air instead of a stuffy parlor. What must Annie think of him?

Mrs. Rollins came back into the room, her mouth set in a firm line. "I don't usually pry into other people's affairs, Mr. Baker, but unseemly behavior by my employees could reflect badly on my business."

"Ma'am." Dallas stood on wobbly legs. "I can assure you it is not how Miss Flannery has made it seem. We were in plain view of several guests on the front porch of the El Tovar." He thought it wise to leave out the part about sitting in the shadows. He'd paid the price for that decision by fighting off Dottie's advances.

Annie huffed and left to pour the coffee. Instead of filling three mugs, as she would usually do, she brought only one. She plopped it down on the table in front of him, then with a swish of her black dress left him alone with her mother.

Mrs. Rollins sighed. "Have a good evening, Mr. Baker. Please take care of your head and try not to sleep for at least an hour to make sure you don't have a concussion." She followed her daughter, leaving Dallas alone.

Feeling like a cad, he lowered himself back into the chair and stared at the dark liquid in his cup, then pushed it away. He didn't want coffee. He wanted sleep, and he'd managed to alienate the two women who could care for him while he stayed awake for an hour.

A few minutes later he wrapped his fingers around his cup, pushed himself to his feet and headed for the front porch. He sat on a rocker, choosing to keep it still so as to not jar his head. He stared at the millions of stars overhead. How could he fix this particular mess?

Dottie obviously thought she had some ownership over him, and that bothered Annie. He sipped his coffee, not ashamed to admit to himself that he rather liked the idea Annie might be jealous.

He needed to pay more attention to how she acted around him. He'd always thought she looked at him as the means to an end. Someone who would take her down into the canyon. Was it possible she viewed him as something more? Then why encourage him to spend time with Dottie? Because that's exactly what she'd done. Women sure were confusing creatures.

What would Pa do in this situation? Most likely, he'd never let himself get between two sparring women in the first place. Dallas shook his head. He didn't care for Dottie other than appreciating her pretty face, and he enjoyed Annie's company. A lot. If only she measured up to what he wanted in a wife, and stopped wearing those stupid skirts.

There was the answer to his questions. He'd write his ma a letter. She was full of Godly wisdom and could give him insight into a woman's mind.

Hopefully, he'd understand the information she gave him, and it wouldn't be like reading another language.

13

"You make a good cup of coffee," Sean told Annie. "Even on a hot summer day, it's a welcome drink. After my travels to the farthest corners of this fine state, your pretty face makes me feel at home."

"Thank you. Have you been preaching to the Indians?" There was no point in telling him every pot tasted the same, whether she made it or someone else. The restaurant was emphatic about having every detail perfect...even the coffee.

"Yes. They're receptive for the most part, although I fear they are mainly humoring me. I'm planning on attending the local church this Sunday. I'd be honored if you'd accompany me."

How could she say no, when she'd be at church, anyway? Thankfully, she was spared giving her answer when Dallas waltzed in. Why didn't he drink his coffee with Mother? It was free over there.

She found her answer when she glanced sideways at the simpering Dottie. How could Annie forget that embarrassing revelation the night before?

"Why don't you sit in Dottie's section?" she said as he came and sat in hers. "She appears to be waiting for you."

Dallas didn't turn his head. "I have no desire to sit there."

"Then why didn't you have your coffee at the boardinghouse?" Annie regretted her snappish tone the moment the words left her lips, but it was too late to pull them back. "I apologize. It's none of my business." Goodness. If Miss Cartwright heard her, she could be terminated on the spot.

"Your mother and Mr. Harris are lost in each other, and I felt like the third wheel." He pressed his lips together. "But if my sitting here offends you, I can move."

"Don't be ridiculous."

Sean's gaze moved from her to Dallas and back again. His eyes widened. "You two seem to be at odds with each other. Is there something I can do?"

"Tell her to stop wearing that split skirt." Dallas set his cup down hard enough for some of the liquid to splash out.

"Tell him to mind his own business and learn to accept people the way they are!" Annie set down the coffeepot and stormed away.

"Dottie, please cover for me," she said as she passed. "I'm not feeling well." She pushed through the kitchen and hurried outside, not stopping until she reached the rim of the canyon.

Of all the infuriating, small-minded...well, a good

Christian woman couldn't really voice how Annie felt at that moment. Tears stung her eyes, and she swiped the back of her hand viciously across her face.

She shouldn't care what Dallas thought, but she did. She sat on a bench provided by the hotel so guests could view the canyon's beauty at their leisure. Taking deep, slow breaths she waited for God to calm her.

Thankfully, His peace and a reassurance of His love and acceptance didn't take long to dry her tears. She had a job to do, and regardless of whether she liked Dottie or not, it wasn't fair to leave the girl to do all the work.

"Annie?" Miss Cartwright bustled toward her. "Are you feeling poorly?"

"Just a touch of nausea. It's passing." Annie grimaced. While not exactly a lie, it wasn't the whole truth, either. "I'm returning to my post."

Miss Cartwright studied her face. "I'd send you home, but another girl up and got married last night. One of the drink girls. Maybe you're ready for something new."

Annie's heart skipped a beat. "Really? I was hoping to discuss that very thing with you later."

"As long as you realize how important a job it is. We can't leave our guests with nothing to wet their whistle, so to speak." She put an arm around Annie's waist. "Come on inside and don't worry about what a couple of fools say."

"You heard?"

"Dear, anyone within ten feet heard. Mr. Laurence ordered me to talk to you about your behavior. Consider yourself spoken to." She squeezed. "Now, let's finish up today and tomorrow you start as drink girl."

"Thank you." Annie sniffed back fresh tears.

"God will take care of your heart's desire, dear girl. Just give him time."

Annie breathed a sigh of relief when she returned to her position and found Dallas and Sean were both gone. She needed several hours, if not a day, before seeing either of them again.

Dottie glared at her and flounced to the opposite end of the counter. Annie didn't care to converse with her, either. Having finished almost three months on the job, Annie was counting down to taking over the Rollins' business and implementing her new ideas.

She might not be getting married, but she did have something that would hopefully support her in her spinsterhood. Sadness bowed her shoulders. Maybe the chance of a future with a husband and children was worth hanging up the split skirt and letting go of some of her strong-minded ways. She'd definitely pray about the possibility.

With the breakfast crowd dispersing, she leaned her elbows on the counter and watched several family groups leave the restaurant. Little girls who looked like their mothers, boys with tousled hair. She sighed and started the cleanup.

Life was too confusing. Most women Annie's age were already settled down. She scrubbed at a dried spot of gravy on the polished wood. Why did folks automatically assume an unmarried woman of nineteen would remain that way? Who set the magical age of twenty as crossing the line into less appealing prospects? Why, men could be as old as twenty-five and have no one breathing down their necks to wed.

Annie had her prospects, of course. She received

several proposals a day from drifters and those riding the rails. None of them set her heart to racing or her blood to boiling like…oh. She put a hand to her mouth.

None of them affected her the way Dallas did. What in the world was she to do?

*

Dallas brushed Rascal's coat. He'd messed up for sure this time. Not wanting a lot of folks to see him with Dottie and start talking, which led to trouble in the shadows, then voicing his opinions about women's attire to a virtual stranger. He'd disappointed Annie and hurt her feelings, and he had no idea how to fix the problem. He needed to write his mother a letter.

After caring for his horse and the mules, he went inside the house in search of paper and ink. Mrs. Rollins was waiting on two men who wanted to book rooms. From the looks of their worn, but clean, clothing, Dallas could hazard a guess they couldn't afford El Tovar.

He stood to the side and waited until Mrs. Rollins escorted the men to their rooms. "May I help you, Mr. Baker?"

"I'm wondering whether you have some stationery and ink I could borrow. I'd like to write my mother a letter."

"What a wonderful idea. You should invite her to visit. We've plenty of room." Mrs. Rollins reached under the boardinghouse's front desk and pulled out a pine box. "Everything you need is right here. Feel free to use the desk in the parlor. Oh, and the two guests that just arrived would like you to take them to the canyon floor tomorrow."

"Yes, ma'am." Wonderful news, considering that he

got paid only when he gave a tour. Mrs. Rollins offered him free room and meals, but his cash income came from guiding.

After seating himself at the polished rolltop desk, Dallas inserted a new tip into the pen and pulled out a sheet of sage-green paper. Fancy. At the top was a monogram with Rollins Boardinghouse. He smiled. Maybe they should offer free paper and ink in each room so guests would be encouraged to write letters and spread the word. He'd mention it to Annie, if she was still speaking to him.

For the first time in months, he poured out his heart to his mother in written words instead of spoken, even going so far as to tell her what a mess he'd made of his friendship with a feisty young lady. He folded the letter and inserted it into an envelope before he could change his mind. Ma always had a way of looking at things that made sense. How would he survive until she replied?

He returned the box to the shelf under the front counter and headed to the mercantile down the road, which also served as a postal and telegraph office. A telegram would be quicker, but too costly to say all that needed saying.

After handing over his letter to the mercantile owner, he stepped back into the sunshine. He needed to stop at El Tovar and leave a message with the concierge about the tour.

Oftentimes the man would put in a word to a few of their guests and generate more business for Dallas, which also allowed the guests to sample Mrs. Rollins's cooking, which advertised her business. It was a good plan for everyone involved, except for maybe the big hotel, which might lose guests due to the more personalized service of Mrs. Rollins. He grinned. Which was the plan.

He approached the desk, catching a glimpse of Annie as she discussed table arrangements with a dark-haired girl. He wanted very much to tell her of his plans, but until she made a move toward renewing their friendship, he'd hold back. After offending her sensibilities, he wouldn't impose.

"Good afternoon, Jenkins." Dallas shook hands with his friend. "I've got a tour heading out tomorrow and have room for four more."

"I know of some men that might be interested. Leaving at sunup as usual?"

Dallas nodded. "It's a quick trip. Back on the third day. One day of fishing in the river. I appreciate whatever you can do."

"Sure thing. There are guests here who prefer not playing billiards or looking at art all the time. I'm sure I'll find someone to send your way."

Dallas's gaze crashed into Annie's as he turned to leave. Her face paled. He forced a smile, then rushed outside, his heart racing like a dirt devil across the desert.

He needed to apologize and had no idea how. Dodging a woman with a broom who was busy sweeping the front porch, he leaped off the stairs and took off at a fast pace, back to the mules. If he was taking a tour out in the morning, even for two men, he needed to make sure all the gear was in good repair. Besides, the mules were easy to understand.

The sounds and odors of the barn soothed him. There was something about being with God's simpler creatures that helped a man get his mind working right.

He doled out the mules' feed, then let them in from the small corral. He'd need to check all their hooves and harnesses, make sure the packs were without holes or rips, and plan the food they'd need for the next few days.

At least the busyness would keep his mind off Annie.

14

Fourth of July, and the dining room was hopping with more than train passengers. It seemed as if folks from all around wanted to see fireworks over the Grand Canyon. Annie smiled. The hotel filled up, and the boardinghouse was full, too. To make matters more festive, hotel management had agreed to close the dining room after the supper crowd, thus allowing the staff to enjoy the celebration.

She rolled the drinks cart between the tables, eyeing the position of the guests' cups and glasses in order to determine, without asking them again, what their preference was. She much preferred her new position over the lunch counter. While she still interacted with the hotel patrons, she didn't have to engage in conversation. She cast a glance toward the counter.

Dallas was nursing his usual morning cup of coffee there, his shoulders hunched over the bar. He'd just returned the night before from another canyon tour, and looked exhausted. With their schedules, they'd not had time for more than "Have a nice day" or "Good evening." She sighed, missing their easy, companionable conversations.

Although he didn't appear to be spending time with Dottie, either, Annie wondered whether he was too busy to pass time with anyone. She felt better at the thought.

"No, I've changed my mind." The woman sitting at the table before her waved a hand. "I no longer want water. Pour me some tea, please."

"Certainly." Annie set the water pitcher back on the tray and reached for the tea. "May I get you anything else?"

"No, that's enough." The woman was alone. While she wore a stylish lavender suit, the lines alongside her thin lips were pronounced, and she seemed lonely.

"Are you enjoying this part of the country on your own?" Annie poured her tea.

She expelled a sharp breath. "Not that it's any of your concern, but yes. I have never married and must travel this great country of ours alone. I've always wanted to see the Grand Canyon, and have the means to do so. I don't need a man to bring me here."

Annie's hands shook and she gripped the cart handle. "You are completely correct." She forced her trembling lips to keep their smile. Was she looking at her future? She tried to detect a trace of beauty under the woman's dour expression. Annie was far from homely. Though she was taller than most women, a large man wouldn't mind overly much.

She glanced again at Dallas, then at Sean, who'd stepped into the room. She wanted to attend the festivities on the arm of a man. Since she had no idea how to mend the rift between herself and Dallas, she'd choose Sean to be her partner. She steered the cart toward him. "Mr. McMurray?"

Ignoring the fact that Dallas had turned on his stool, she proceeded. "I accept your invitation to tonight's festivities."

His eyes widened, most likely because he'd not actually asked her to join him. She prayed he'd go along with her ploy. Maybe a touch of jealousy would open Dallas's mouth so he could utter an apology for his outrageous behavior.

"I'm honored, Miss Rollins." The pastor nodded. "I'll meet you in front of your home at dusk."

She squared her shoulders, tossed Dallas a grin she knew was a childish gesture, then sashayed to the kitchen to refill her pitchers. On her way back out, she ran the cart into Dottie, who was rushing in. The other girl bent over, her breath leaving in a whoosh.

"You…did…that on purpose." She straightened and glared. "You're mad because I'm going to the celebration with Dallas."

"You are?" What did Annie expect? She'd acted like a wanton fool in front of the man, all but daring him to find an escort of his own. "That's nice." She pushed past the other girl and back into the dining room.

Dottie followed. "I'm going to marry that man, you know. He owns a ranch and can give me the life I've always dreamed of having."

"Has he proposed?" Annie whirled.

Dottie smiled, her green eyes glittering. "Not yet," she whispered. "But a little more coercing and we'll be hitched in no time."

"You're trying to seduce him!" Annie hissed and grabbed her arm, dragging her into the corner. "That is immoral and unfair."

Dottie lifted her chin. "Why should you care? You're chasing after the handsome pastor."

"I am not doing anything remotely similar to your actions." Catching the eye of Miss Cartwright, Annie moved back to her cart. She needed to find a way to warn Dallas. After all, they were friends, even though estranged at the moment. It was her place to warn him of the other girl's evil intentions.

She met his gaze across the room. Her heart did an odd flip-flop. More and more lately her body betrayed her with feelings and reactions toward Dallas that left her confused. If she wasn't careful, she might actually think she carried romantic notions about him.

That would never do. Not with his preconceived notions about women.

She tore her gaze away and went back to concentrating on her job. The harder she worked, the faster the day would pass. Instead of dwelling on Dallas, she'd focus on the new clothes Mother had made, which hung in her room. A sunshine-yellow skirt that complimented her hair and eyes, and a fresh white blouse with a ribbon around the neck that matched the skirt. For the first time in a long time, Annie was excited about clothes other than her split skirt.

She cast another glance at Dallas. What would he think of her when he saw her in the new outfit? Would his eyes light up in appreciation? She hoped so.

Maybe, after tonight, he'd notice that a woman could wear split skirts and still be feminine.

*

Dallas couldn't believe he'd asked Dottie to the celebration that evening. He sure was a glutton for punishment. Well, the harm was done. He'd have to make sure they were in full sight of other partygoers at all times. He slapped his hat against his thigh as he made his way to the barn.

If Annie hadn't tossed him that challenging grin, he wouldn't have succumbed to stupidity. He banged open the barn door, wincing when it slammed against the wall. Just because he was tired and out of sorts didn't give him rein to break something that didn't belong to him, and that he'd have to fix in the end. Maybe a short nap in the straw would improve his mood.

The tour ending the day before had been a humdinger. One of the three men had sneaked in a bottle of whiskey, despite the rules of no liquor allowed. Things had almost turned violent when Dallas struggled with the guest over the bottle. Luckily, a drunk man was unsteady on his feet. The incident resulted in little sleep for Dallas as he remained on the alert for other broken rules.

Now, he'd spend an evening fending off Dottie's advances. He groaned and grabbed a curry brush from the shelf. Brushing Rascal was the best thing to calm him. That and prayer. He sent off several while grooming his horse. The main prayer being that he wouldn't be caught in a compromising position with the grabby Miss Flannery.

He should've swallowed his pride and asked Annie to accompany him to watch fireworks. All it would have taken was a simple apology and an explanation about what had really happened. But embarrassment held him back. Now, he potentially could find himself in the same situation. He needed to stay away from El Tovar. Trouble resided between those log walls, and two very pretty Harvey waitresses.

He'd checked for mail every day, waiting for a response from Ma. He sorely needed her wise counsel.

When Rascal's coat gleamed from the attention, Dallas replaced the brush and laid in a fresh pile of straw. He definitely needed a nap.

When he awoke, the shadows through the barn door alerted him that it was late afternoon. He bolted to his feet and rushed through the house and upstairs to his room. He might not be excited about an evening with Dottie, but he had asked her and couldn't be late.

After washing in the basin and donning clean clothes, Dallas made it to the hotel just as the girls were emerging from the building. Annie wasn't with them. But of course, she wouldn't be. She lived at home and would get ready there.

Dottie looked pretty in a green blouse and black skirt. Dallas offered her his arm. "There is a vendor selling ice cream. Would you like one?"

"That sounds divine." She clutched his arm with both hands, pressing herself uncomfortably close.

Dallas sighed. He'd definitely make sure they stayed in a throng of celebrators.

After they purchased ice cream and sat at a makeshift table of boards placed over logs, Dallas glanced around. At least fifty people milled around the vendors selling not only ice cream, but toys and handmade crafts. It looked as if almost everyone in town took advantage of the throng of tourists to make a few extra dollars. Even a few Indian women had spread a blanket with turquoise jewelry.

His ma and sisters would love a necklace. If he purchased something for them, would Dottie expect a trinket also? Most likely, and probably a ring. No, he'd have to settle for paying a little extra at the mercantile for his gifts.

"I can't wait for the fireworks." Dottie licked her spoon with the daintiness of a cat, her eyes narrowing. "I've never seen any before."

"Never?" He focused on his bowl, trying not to notice the sultry looks she sent his way. "Then you're in for a treat."

"The real treat is sitting beside you on a blanket." She winked.

Dallas choked. Maybe he could pretend to get ill. Ah. Maybe there was something he could do to make the woman lose interest.

Annie strolled in their direction, her arm linked lightly with McMurray's. Dallas's jaw dropped. She was a vision in yellow.

"Good evening, Dallas. Dottie." She nodded her lovely head in their direction.

Dallas's mouth dried up, leaving Dottie to answer. "Good evening. You should try the ice cream. Very creamy." She licked her lips.

Dallas could feel the blood rush from his head to his feet. His eyes widened as he locked gazes with Annie. She set her lips firmly and tugged Sean away.

Surely she didn't think he welcomed Dottie's forward actions. He shoved aside what was left of his ice cream. Fool. He couldn't even return her greeting. Not after the first glimpse of her looking as pretty as a sunset.

When had he started looking at Annie as a woman rather than a friend? Was that why he had a hard time admitting his faults and apologizing?

A young boy sped past, yelling out that the fireworks were starting. Dallas pushed to his feet and offered Dottie his hand. Maybe the simple gesture would keep her from pressing her body against his. Or maybe not, judging from the beaming smile on her face.

Did holding hands signify something he didn't know about? He really should've questioned his ma more about the workings of a woman's mind. His younger sister probably had more wisdom in courting than he did.

Dottie dragged him toward a quilt next to the one Annie shared with her beau. Dallas exchanged nods with McMurray, then lowered himself beside Dottie. Normally, he reclined back on his elbows. Not tonight. That would put him at the mercy of an unscrupulous woman.

15

Annie sat with a straight posture next to Sean. What she wanted to do was wear her split skirt and recline back in a more comfortable position. The fireworks would start any second, and she already had a crick in her neck.

The first riot of color exploded over the canyon. Sean inched his hand over Annie's. She sighed and brushed a piece of lint from her dress, as if she hadn't noticed. He scooted closer, and she shifted away. Obviously, the man thought their relationship was further along than she did. When his elbow connected with hers and she ran out of quilt, Annie rolled her eyes and decided to enjoy the fireworks show.

After all, the man was a pastor. He wouldn't get too forward, would he? She cut him a sideways glance. He was too close.

"There's a hayride after." Sean's breath tickled her

ear. "Would you like a ride?"

Her first instinct was to say no, but Dottie's giggle drifted across the short distance, deciding for her. "Yes, thank you."

The fireworks lasted only a few minutes, but that was enough to raise Annie's patriotic spirit. What a fine country they lived in. God had blessed their great land with freedom. Where a person could follow her dreams and become whatever she wanted. Annie glanced toward the dark canyon. Well, almost.

She accepted Sean's help to her feet. They'd taken two steps when Annie heard a cry, then a scream. She whirled.

A woman fell to her knees at the edge of the canyon. "My boy! He's fallen over. Help him, somebody, please."

Annie let go of Sean and hitched up her dress. He shot out a hand to stop her. "Wait, Annie. Let me."

"It'll take all of us, Sean. If it's not already too late." She shook him off and continued, as Dallas shot past her.

"Get some rope!" He pulled the woman away from the edge. "Someone care for this lady. Annie?"

"The barn." Annie gave Sean a shove. He nodded and dashed away.

Annie gathered the distraught woman in her arms, until Mother arrived to take over. Once she was there, coaxing a cup of coffee into the other mother's hands, Annie moved next to Dallas. "Thank God the moon is bright. Can you see him?"

"Not yet. Could you gather some lanterns?" He dropped to his hands and knees, then his stomach, to peer over the edge. "It might not help much, but light seems to lift folks' spirits."

If anyone could save the child, Dallas could. Annie had no doubt. She headed to the barn, spreading word about needing lanterns as she went. When she met Sean coming back, she took the rope from him and directed him into the house to collect every lamp he could find.

She returned, to hand the rope to Dallas. "Anything?"

"I'm not sure." He scooted back and stood. "I think I see something white on a ledge." He shook his head. "I don't need to tell you what happened to that poor child if he missed a ledge."

Tears clogged her throat, but she couldn't give in to them. Not yet. "Then we'll pray he didn't miss." She gripped Dallas's arms. "We'll pray that he has nothing but minor injuries and is sitting there, waiting for you to save him."

Dallas gave a sad smile. "Know for a fact I'm the one to go, do you?"

"There's no one more qualified. No one stronger." Realizing she'd stepped closer to him than was seemly, she moved back, her face heating. One deep breath from both of them and they would have brushed chests. What must he think of her? "God will help you."

"Oh, Dallas." Dottie squeezed between them. "I've never been so frightened in my life. Please take me back to the hotel. I feel faint."

"Are you serious?" Annie crossed her arms. "A boy could be dying, and you're afraid I'm getting too close to your beau. If you're going to faint, there are still plenty of blankets on the ground."

"Wait." Dallas held up his hand. "We aren't—"

Dottie spun to face Annie. "Maybe you should go back to yours!"

"Everything all right here?" Sean set four lanterns on the ground at their feet. "Mr. Baker?"

"We're fine." He bent and retrieved the lamps. "I could use some help shedding light, both physically and spiritually, it seems."

"Sean and I will both help." Annie glared at Dottie. "Go back to your room. You're no help here."

The other girl opened and closed her mouth a few times, then finally snapped it shut. With a swish of her skirt, she stomped away. Good riddance. Annie shook her head. How could the girl be so selfish? A child might be dying, and there they stood arguing—no, fighting—over Dallas. Shame heated Annie's face.

What if their delay cost the child his life? She'd never be able to live with herself.

By now, Dallas was tying the rope around his waist, as Sean and other men lit lanterns and placed them along the canyon edge. The lamps lit up the immediate area but did little to illuminate the expanse into which Dallas would have to lower himself. He grabbed another coiled rope and looped it over his shoulder. Three men held tight to one end of it.

Dallas's lips moved silently. The fact he prayed both lifted and lowered Annie's hopes. He could be praying he found the boy alive or that the mother would be able to deal with her loss. Their chances of recovering anything other than a dead body, if they could recover it, were very slim.

Sean and Pastor Carson called for everyone to join hands. "Father, we come to You, asking for Your guiding hand as Dallas steps over the ledge into the danger of the canyon. We pray for his protection and that of the young boy Billy. Please return the child to his mother and Dallas to us. In the name of Your son, Jesus, we pray. Amen."

*

Dallas hung backward over the canyon edge while several men held the other end of the rope. This was it.. His gaze clashed with Annie's. He studied every line of her beautiful face, knowing very well it might be the last thing he ever saw.

He accepted a lantern handed to him by Pastor Carson, flashed what he hoped was a reassuring grin at Annie, then slowly lowered himself over the rim, the men holding the other end feeding him the rope inch by inch.

"Dallas." Annie fell to her knees, bringing her face to the same level as his. "Please, be careful."

He wanted to draw her close for a kiss, feel her lips against his in case he never had another chance. He figured that would get him slapped the moment he stepped foot back on solid ground. "I will." Keeping his gaze locked on hers, he continued to lower himself until her face was nothing but a pale blur above him.

"Billy?" he called into the inky blackness. "I need you to talk to me, buddy. Tell me where you are." Please God, let him be able to speak. "Billy!"

"I'm here, mister." A voice, faint but unmistakable, came from Dallas's lower right.

"Don't move, son. Keep an eye out for me. You'll see me before I see you. Don't let me pass you."

"I won't."

With each rappel, the boy's voice sounded clearer. Thank God he was alive. Now to keep him that way. "Are you hurt?"

"My head is bleeding, and I think I broke my arm."

"How old are you?" Keep him talking; that's what folks always did in these types of situations, right?

"Ten. Today is my birthday. Ma is going to be furious. She told me to stay away from the edge, but I thought I was old enough for a better look."

Dallas chuckled, remembering all the times he'd disobeyed as a kid. None of them had turned out all right. In fact, several resulted in a switch across his bottom.

He stopped on a narrow ledge about a hundred feet from the top. The boy sat pressed against the rock face, his arm cradled in his lap. "Son, I reckon your ma is going to hug you more than anything. She's that worried."

Uncoiling the extra strand of rope, Dallas did his best to assess the situation in the dark. First off, they needed a sling for the boy's arm. He doubted Billy could handle taking off his own shirt. It would hurt something fierce. So Dallas unbuttoned his own. People would have to accept him without his shirt for a few minutes. "I'm going to tie this around your arm. We'll have to keep it as secure as possible. It won't feel good when they drag you to the top, but there isn't a lot of help for it."

"I can handle it." The boy's voice shook despite his brave words.

"I'm sure you can, being a grown boy of ten." Dallas's foot slipped on a loose rock, reminding him how precarious their situation was. "Let's get this tied around your waist." He set the lantern against the cliff face, and then felt around the ground, realizing the ledge was maybe three to four feet wide. How in the world had the boy stopped on such a small bit of rock?

Dallas's fingers came into contact with a stick about two inches in diameter.

"As tough as you are, son, you'll still need to bite down on this." Once the second rope was secured around Billy's waist, Dallas jerked on it with two hands, his signal for them to pull the youngster to safety.

Billy cried out with the first jerk. Hopefully, he wouldn't pass out from the pain. The men above needed whatever help the poor boy could give them.

Dallas leaned back to watch the child ascend. As he did so, his feet slipped.

His arms windmilled and he fell backward into space. The rope cut into his waist, so sharply it knocked the air from his lungs. Dallas swung back and forth, then slammed against the rock face, headfirst. It seemed like an eternity before he stopped swinging..

His heart beat hard enough that he heard it in his ears. He placed a hand on his forehead, where he'd hit the rocks, and took it away sticky. Wonderful. He had another wound for Annie to stitch. Of course, the bang on his head might be the least of his worries, especially since the rope wasn't moving. What were the other men doing up there?

He glanced up. The rope was wedged between two rocks. He tried getting traction on the canyon wall, but since the ledge hung over, his legs wouldn't reach. He braced his feet against the cliff and pushed, swinging like a pendulum, angling his body so his back took the hits instead of his face. After what seemed like eons, the rope started to move. The sharp edge of the ledge rubbed the strands, and Dallas prayed they wouldn't cut through. It was a long fall to the canyon floor, and he doubted a man his size would be lucky enough to find a ledge big enough to catch him.

Inch by agonizing inch, he felt himself being pulled upward. He'd have plenty of scrapes and bruises when he arrived, and he couldn't help but feel some pleasure at imagining Annie tending to him. Annie with her soft hands and fresh scent.

He shook his head, then grimaced at the wooziness that assailed him. He must've hit his head harder than he'd thought. Finally, his shoulders cleared the canyon rim, and he was dragged over the top until he lay in the grass and pine needles.

Annie rushed to his side, smoothing his hair back from his face. "You're a hero, Dallas Baker. A true hero." She looked at her fingers. "And you're bleeding."

"Yep. Guess I am." Dallas closed his eyes. "I'm going to sleep now."

"No, sir, you are not. Sean, help me get him to his feet."

He was tugged and pulled until he stood. The world spun as hands grappled at his waist, struggling to remove a rope cinched tight. "I'm done." Dallas pitched face-first to the ground.

16

Annie wiped a cool wet cloth across Dallas's forehead, trying not to watch as Mother dabbed witch hazel on the scrapes across his rib cage and chest. Annie's face burned. When Mother had told her she'd need her help tending to Dallas after the doc taped his broken ribs, she'd thought she would melt into the floor.

Now, she struggled to avert her eyes from something she had no right to see. If she did drop her gaze from his face, Mother cleared her throat with the fierceness of a mountain lion. Annie let a small smile tug at her lips. Improper behavior and embarrassment or not, she'd managed a small glance. The sight had taken her breath away.

"Go heat some water, Annie, and quit staring. The poor man isn't on display at the mercantile. We'll make him some tea."

Annie dropped her cloth into the porcelain bowl. She

seriously doubted whether Dallas wanted tea. Coffee seemed to be his drink of choice.

She headed down the stairs. Two men and a woman waited in front of the small reception counter. "May I help you?" Annie wiped her damp hands on her apron.

"Ma'am." A man in a bowler hat stepped aside and waved the woman forward.

"Thank you, sir. My name is Ellen Baker. I believe my son lives and works here?"

Annie pressed her lips together to prevent her mouth from falling open. Since Dallas's father had failed to bring him home, had the family sent his mother? "I'm Annie Rollins. We're happy to have you. One moment and I will show you to your room."

Gracious. How would she ever tell her that her son lay upstairs unconscious?

Mrs. Baker nodded. "I'll wait in the parlor while you take care of these gentlemen. I'm in no hurry." She hid a yawn behind a gloved hand. "The railroad ran late. Sorry to impose upon you at this advanced hour."

"It's no trouble Mrs. Baker." As the woman moved to the parlor, Annie smiled and opened the registry book for the men to sign. Mother would be thrilled with the business. Two paying guests. Neither she nor Annie would consider letting Mrs. Baker pay for her room, though. "There we go." She handed each of the men a key and directed them to their rooms.

Taking a deep breath, she marched into the parlor, ready to tell Mrs. Baker about her heroic son and the subsequent injuries. Hopefully, she wouldn't find the boardinghouse at fault.

"Ma'am." Annie twisted her apron.

"Yes?" Mrs. Baker turned from the window.

"Well, um, it's about Dallas." She bit her lip.

"Is he no longer here? Has he headed back to Texas?" Mrs. Baker shook her head. "I was afraid his father might have used more force than necessary. I tell the man all the time that our sons need to find their own way in the world."

"No, ma'am, I mean, yes, he's still here." Oh, she was a bumbling idiot. "A small child fell into the canyon tonight. Dallas went after him, and now he's unconscious upstairs, with a concussion and broken ribs."

The other woman arched an eyebrow. "Dallas or the child?"

"Dallas."

She nodded. "That sounds like my boy, heading off to someone's aid. Please take me to him."

"Yes, ma'am." Annie rushed to lead the way. She stopped in front of Dallas's room and waved his mother in before her. "Mother, this is Mrs. Baker, Dallas's mother."

Mother looked taken aback before regaining her composure and stepping forward. "It's a pleasure to meet you. I'm Esther Rollins."

"Ellen." Mrs. Baker dropped her reticule on the foot of the bed, then perched beside her son. "He's quite battered, isn't he?" She wrung out the cloth Annie had dropped earlier.

"And quite the hero. You should be very proud of him." Mother handed her the witch hazel and cotton. "Would you like some tea while you care for your son?"

"That would be delightful."

Mother ushered Annie from the room. "Is the water

boiling?"

"No. We have two other guests, also. I planned on putting Mrs. Baker in the rose room, but we never made it that far."

"Quite right. A mother always wants to be with her child when that child has been injured." Mother grabbed the teakettle. "See if there are any of those cookies left from this morning. It may be late, but that poor woman must be famished."

Annie followed orders automatically. Her heart lay like a cold stone in the pit of her stomach. Mrs. Baker would take Dallas home for sure. He might be a grown man, but men tended to listen to their mothers, even if no one else. She'd miss him. Very much. Life at the Grand Canyon would never be the same.

Maybe Annie should consider leaving. She could renew her contract with the Harvey Company and head east or to California. Instead of a sea of sand, she could gaze upon an ocean of wonder. With Mother marrying Mr. Harris, she doubted it would take too much convincing to get her to sell the house. Annie suspected she kept it running for her daughter's future, in case she never married.

Could Annie leave one of God's greatest wonders for the unknown? She doubted she'd see anything as grand as the canyon in the towns along the railroad tracks. But she wouldn't know unless she tried.

She located the cookies and set them on a tray. If she remained with the Harvey Company, she could travel and eventually settle wherever she wanted. If she decided to return to the area, she could possibly be head waitress at El Tovar someday. She set the tray next to the stove and moved to the window, where she gazed out into the night.

Yes, if everyone she cared about was no longer there in Williams, she could be convinced to leave her home.

*

"Ma?" Dallas struggled to sit up. Pain shot down his side, stealing his breath. "How long have I been down? Am I dying? What are you doing here?"

She laughed and placed a hand on his shoulder. "Stay still, son. No, you aren't dying, and since I just arrived, I have no idea how long you've been lying here, but I suspect only an hour or two." She slid another pillow behind him. "See if you can't take a sip of tea, all right?"

"Then why are you here?" He craned his neck to drink.

"I came as quick as the train would bring me in response to your letter." She set the cup on a bedside table and frowned. "I thought I taught you better than I obviously did."

"How so?" His breath hitched. "Did I bust some ribs?"

She nodded. "Yes, and I'm very proud of your heroic action, but if not for your saving of that young boy's life, I'd box your ears. Have another sip of tea."

"I don't want any tea." Dallas groaned. "Ma. Why. Are. You. Here? Did Pa send you?"

"Of course your pa didn't send me. I have a mind of my own, and so, it seems, does the young lady you apparently have your eye on." Ma smiled. "Was that the blonde one who brought me up here? She's lovely. And no sight of a split skirt."

"She's very lovely." Dallas closed his eyes, took a deep breath, then opened them again, ready for a lecture. "When she isn't wearing that skirt."

"What difference does that make?" Ma's eyes shot sparks.

"I want a wife who's a lady like you." He shifted. Why couldn't he get comfortable? "A woman who doesn't mind some hard work, but still looks like a lady."

Ma pounded the mattress, sending a shard of pain through his ribs. "I apologize to you for raising a fool." She stood. "I'll be back in the morning, and pray you grow some wisdom in the meantime."

"Wait." Dallas struggled halfway to a sitting position and supported his weight on his elbow. "I'm thoroughly confused." Why wouldn't she answer his questions? Why did she keep calling him a fool? Ma had always been loving and supportive, kind but firm.

She heaved a sigh. "Son, I've been wearing split skirts for years. I even have a leather one with fringe. We do live on a ranch, where a dress or full skirt is impractical." She placed a kiss on his forehead. "Think about it. You'll remember. But even if I didn't occasionally have the need to dress less femininely, that is no reason for a son of mine to pass up a good thing because of prejudice. Good night, son." She glided from the room, leaving him alone.

Ma wore the slimmer, split skirts? He laid back and stared at the ceiling. Had he been so busy working with the cattle and horses he'd never really noticed what she wore? Had he only assumed?

His head hurt, impeding his thought processes. If Ma said she wore those infernal skirts, then she must. She'd never lie to him. He closed his eyes and pulled the sheet up around his chin.

When he awoke the next morning, sunlight streamed through the open curtains, and Annie was placing a tray on the bedside table. "Good morning." She smiled. "Feeling better?"

"Some." He yanked the sheet back into place. "Where's my mother?"

"Having breakfast. You're a big boy. You don't need her around every moment." Annie fluffed his pillows, tantalizing him with a flowery scent. She wore her uniform, most likely taking care of his needs before heading to work.

"You're late."

She nodded. "I let them know. Folks around here think you can walk on water after what you did. No one will care that I'm late, because I brought your breakfast. Do you need anything else?"

He shook his head and watched her leave, the black skirt swishing around her ankles, the white ribbon bobbing in her puffed-up hair. She was lovely in her uniform, beautiful in anything else. Yes, he was a fool.

"Mr. Baker?" The boy he'd rescued the night before peered around the door frame. "Can I come in? The woman downstairs said it was okay."

"Sure, Billy." Dallas pushed himself to a sitting position. "I'm glad for the company. You can hand me that brown shirt over there."

The boy handed him the garment, and Dallas slipped his arms through the sleeves. He was tired of going shirtless in a houseful of women. Besides, no more bed rest for him. He planned to be up and about within the hour.

"How are you feeling, Billy? How's the arm?"

Billy showed him the cast. "Only hurts a little bit,

now. My ma said pain is good. It's proof that I'm alive."

"That it does." Dallas grimaced. He was living big time, judging by the pain coursing through his head and body. The child should be pretty banged up, too. He marveled at the resilience of a ten-year-old boy.

"I brought you something," Billy said, darting back into the hall. When he arrived, he had a crate in his hand. A whimpering came from inside. "I snuck it in, but the lady in black caught me. She said it was okay." Billy pulled out a yellow pup and set it in Dallas's lap. "I want you to have my puppy as thanks for saving me. I'll get one out of the neighbor man's next litter."

Mrs. Rollins would have a fit. Dallas laughed as the pup clambered up and licked his face. "What's his name?"

"Whatever you want it to be. I was kind of thinking Hero, like you." Billy climbed onto the bed. "Tell me if I jostle you too much or the puppy hurts you. I thought he could keep you company until you're up and about."

Dallas didn't feel like a hero. He'd done what any person would, but he did love animals. And this little furry Hero had hair the same color as Annie's.

17

The room erupted in applause.

Annie turned. She almost dropped the full carafe of coffee. "What are you doing out of bed?" Dallas and his mother were seated at one of her tables.

He gave a small wave around the room, his face bright, and pulled out a chair for Mrs. Baker. "I'm feeling fine and wanted to share a special meal with Ma." He sat across the table from his mother.

"But your head. Your ribs." Annie poured them both cups of coffee. "You shouldn't overdo things."

Mrs. Baker placed a hand over hers. "I'll see he's careful. Don't fret."

Shame burned up Annie's neck and into her face. "I apologize. Of course you know what's best for your son." She couldn't push the cart to the next table fast enough. How could she be so dense as to berate Dallas in front of his mother? No one knew better than she what he needed.

Annie rushed through the kitchen and into the pantry. She leaned against the wall and closed her eyes. Lord, have mercy on her for her foolishness. She'd lost all reason where Dallas was concerned.

Her heart almost stopped as she relived the moment he'd keeled over into the dirt. Thinking him dead, she'd fallen to her knees at his side and ranted like a madwoman. From the astonished look on Sean's face, she doubted he'd ask to spend time with her again. Mother hadn't missed the show of emotion on Annie's part, either. Luckily, Dottie had already returned to the hotel in a huff by then, and Annie had been spared her dramatics. Maybe she could play off the moment as extreme concern for a dear friend and nothing more.

"Shirking your duties?" Dottie squeezed into the room. "People are waiting for their drinks."

Annie sighed and pushed past her. It wouldn't do for Miss Cartwright, or the hotel manager, to find her slacking. She'd have to dwell on her feelings at night in bed. The only place where she could enjoy a moment of privacy.

Her steps slowed. When was the last time she'd sat in her special place overlooking the canyon? Most likely, that was what she needed to fix what ailed her. Time with God in His glorious creation.

The busyness of life had distracted her from what was really important. Spirits lighter, she entered the dining room and resumed pouring drinks for the customers. Sean sat at one table, and greeted her with a smile. Annie's own smile faltered. She'd thought for sure he'd want nothing more to do with her.

"Good morning, Annie." He nodded toward his

coffee cup. "Seems our local hero has a visitor."

"His mother."

"Perfect timing. Now, neither you nor your mother will have to care for him." He stopped her by placing his hand on her arm. "You have enough to do."

Here was her chance to begin removing any ideas people might have about her feelings for Dallas. "My mother did most of the work before his arrived." Annie set the pitcher back on the tray. "It's difficult to see such a dear friend hurting."

He tilted his head and stared for a few seconds. "A friend?"

"A friend." She forced a smile and moved along the line of tables.

Word should spread soon enough, dispelling any rumors that might be flying around since the night before. If she was lucky, word would reach Mother's ears and she'd actually believe them.

A never-ending stream of customers filled Annie's day. By the time her shift was over, her feet and back ached. She couldn't remember a time the boardinghouse, much less the hotel, had been so full. The railroad benefited everyone.

Still, tired or not, she headed to her seat by the canyon. She removed the bow from her hair and untied her apron, placing both on the log beside her. The canyon plunged into darkness before her, but she'd stared at the view so many times, she had no trouble picturing its beauty. Now, she also saw its danger.

Once Dallas was healed, she'd ask him to put up a railing. It should have been done years ago. They'd been lucky so far that no one had died. But as the area grew more populated and drew more visitors, the risk of accidents increased.

She glanced over her shoulder to see Dallas and his mother approaching the front porch. He helped her into one of the rockers and sat beside her. In her black dress, in the shadows of the pine trees, Annie doubted Dallas could see her.

Instead of peace, she felt alone. Mother had Mr. Harris, Dallas had Dottie and his mother, and Annie had no one. Only Sean on occasion. Maybe she expected too much from people. Was it possible that the calm feelings she experienced around the pastor were what couples felt for each other? Could it be that the racing of her heart when Dallas walked into a room was something fleeting, an emotion that wouldn't stand the test of time?

She picked up a stick and drew patterns in the dirt she couldn't see in the dark. The voices from the porch drifted her way, muffled by the distance. How nice that Dallas had the freedom to converse openly with his mother. Since her husband's death, Mother had become withdrawn. That is until Mr. Harris started paying her attention.

Did a woman need a man to make her complete? Confusion clouded Annie's mind. She wanted to be a man's helpmate, as the Bible said one should be. Not a helpless woman who could do nothing on her own or one who needed a man to make her feel fulfilled. Times were changing, and Annie wanted to adapt to them.

The problem was…she no longer knew whether she wanted to adapt alone or not.

*

"The two of you skirt around each other like territorial bears," Ma said, setting her rocker into motion. "Why don't you go talk to the girl?"

"About what?" Dallas shook his head.

"You could start by thanking her for caring for you after your fall. According to her mother, they both tended to you until I arrived."

Annie had seen him half-dressed. His mouth dried up. No wonder she wouldn't meet his eyes. Could they talk about her tending him without that uncomfortable subject being broached?

"Who is the young Irish girl giving you dog eyes all morning?" Ma brushed at her skirt.

"Just a girl I've kept company with a time or two."

"Hmm."

"What?" Dallas tried to make out her features.

"Don't toy with a girl's affections, son. The way that little lady looks at you, I'm guessing she doesn't see you as an occasional acquaintance."

"I was afraid of that." But then again, she'd left when a man needed a woman. Dallas could tell her that was the reason things couldn't work between them. That she was too young for a man ready to settle down and have a family.

He glanced to where Annie sat, the moon shining on her hair. He would convince that one someday. If she'd listen. He still had a hard time coming to terms with the way Ma said she sometimes dressed. Why did it bother him so much?

"My reluctance to tell Annie how I feel has to be more than her choice of skirts."

"That's not something I can help you with." Ma continued to rock, the chair giving an occasional squeak. "But I'm guessing it might have something to do with your aunt Sadie."

"Who?"

"My sister." Ma grinned. "She's in California somewhere. I get a letter from her once in a while. You haven't seen her since you were a little bitty thing. She made quite the impression, though, with her split skirts, raunchy speech and smelly cigars."

He searched his memory. He had a vague impression of a woman with a long, mahogany-colored braid and a rifle as tall as she was. "Wasn't she a drover?"

"Ah, you do remember. Yes, she still is, and according to her, loved by everyone she runs across."

"Then why did she make an unfavorable impression on me?"

"As the baby in the family at that time, you were frightened by her. Your older brothers thought she was a hoot." Ma chuckled. "She is a strange bird, my sister, but you won't find a woman who loves the Lord more." She patted his hand. "Son, you've got to stop judging people by the way they look. Pray about it. If that little gal is meant for you, then God will make a way."

He nodded. Hero bounded from the barn and made a beeline for Annie.

She laughed, the sound as pretty as a babbling brook. She scooped Hero into her arms and nuzzled him.

Silly mutt with a silly name. "Guess I ought to go fetch my dog."

Ma chuckled again. "Son, I've missed you very much."

He stood and bent to lay a kiss on her cheek. "Not as much as I've missed you. I plan on staying here for a while longer, but I'll return to the ranch someday."

"See that you do." She pushed to her feet. "I'm going to retire to my room now and write your pa a letter telling him I'll be home in a few days. Good night, son."

"Good night, Ma." He watched her enter the house, then he headed toward Annie.

She giggled and fell off the log, Hero in her arms. She glanced up at Dallas. "Hello."

"You've made a friend." He took the dog in one arm, receiving his own share of slobbery kisses, and helped Annie back to her seat with the other.

"He's a darling." She scratched under the puppy's chin. "I've always wanted a dog, but Mother always said no. Is that why you're keeping him in the barn?"

"Yeah. I haven't told her I have him yet."

"Good luck." Annie stood and smoothed her skirts. "It's been a long day. I need to get some sleep. Are you feeling all right? Ribs don't hurt too much?"

"I'm fine." He set Hero on the ground. "Thanks for your help last night."

She turned her face away. "I wish I could've done more. But you're fine, and Billy will grow to be an old man, God willing. Will you be returning to Texas soon?"

"Why would you ask that?" Dallas faced her. "Because Ma is visiting? She's only checking on me, not taking me back with her." He grasped Annie's arm. "Would you mind if I were to go back?"

Still not looking at him, she tried to pull free. "Of course I would. We're friends."

"Friends?" He wasn't sure how he felt about that. The fact she wouldn't look at him gave him hope that she cared more for him than she wanted to admit. "Is that all?"

"That's the best thing to be, isn't it?" She yanked her

hands from his and scooped up Hero, hiding her face behind his furry neck. "You have dreams for your life, I have mine."

"To go to the canyon floor." Yes, he'd heard it before.

"Not just that." Her eyes sparkled in the moonlight. Now she looked at him. "I'm thinking of renewing my contract with the Harvey Company and traveling. I'm not really marriage material, and this will give me a chance to see the nation. Mother and Mr. Harris won't feel obligated to make sure I'm cared for."

"What about the boardinghouse?"

She shrugged. "I'll sell it. While I'm perfectly capable of running it successfully, maybe even competing with the El Tovar in some way, it's not what I want to spend the rest of my life doing, and I've realized I don't have the proper skills to lead tours into the canyon." She blinked rapidly. "I've never even been down there."

Dallas's heart ripped in two, and he prayed he had nothing to do with her believing she wasn't marriage material. How could she be anything else?

18

Annie gave Miss Cartwright a hug, not caring about the Harvey policy against public displays of affection. "I promise I'll let you know as soon as I return."

"No hurry." Miss Cartwright held her at arm's length. "Guests will be fewer once the snows hit. Go have that experience you've been craving."

"Thank you." Annie dashed from the hotel. She'd spent months tiptoeing around Dallas and watching Mother and Mr. Harris move closer to a wedding date, and today was the last tour Dallas would lead into the canyon until springtime. She had to be part of that tour. She might not have another chance.

She glanced at the barn, where he and three men gathered around the mules. Mother was tying a bedroll behind a saddle. Mother? Mr. Harris? Oh, Annie needed to hurry. There was one riding mule left.

The day before, she'd packed warm clothes and

enough food for several days. She grabbed the bedroll and saddlebags from under her bed now and raced back outside, grateful for the slimmer split skirt that afforded her ease of movement.

"Wait! I'm coming." Out of breath, she dropped her bags and darted into the barn.

"What are you doing?" Dallas stepped behind her.

"Getting the mule ready." Annie slipped the bridle over the animal's head. "What does it look like?"

He sighed. "I'll do it. It'll be faster. Good thing there isn't a large group, since the entire family decided to come."

"Oh, I need to put a sign on the door saying we're closed for business." She whirled, only to have Dallas stop her.

"Your mother is taking care of it." He laughed. "You're like a child at Christmas. Are you tagging along because McMurray is coming again?"

"What? No." Gracious. She might have thought twice had she known. No help for it now. Nothing was going to keep her from finally fulfilling her dream. "I want to do this while I decide whether to renew my contract with the Harvey Company."

"That's right. It expired yesterday." Mule ready, Dallas led the beast outside.

"You've kept track?" Warmth spread through her.

"It's all you've talked about for days." His gaze lit on her with humor. He patted her head. "Glad to have you along."

She froze, mouth falling open. Did he just pat her like a dog? She clamped her lips closed and glared. He'd acted as if he was patronizing a younger sister. Well, she'd show him. She'd fend for herself on the trip, asking nothing of him.

Bumping him roughly with her shoulder, she forced her way past him and took the lead to the mule. "Thank you for your help, but it isn't needed." She walked o the others and started tying on her supplies. Smiling, she patted one of the bags, where she'd stashed her father's Bowie knife and pistol. She was perfectly capable of taking care of herself.

"I'm surprised to see you, Mother." Annie cinched the saddle.

"The feeling is mutual." Mother smiled. "Mr. Harris and I thought it would be a nice time together. Help us clear our heads while we decide what to do with the house. You don't seem to want it."

"I haven't decided." Annie knew she wasn't being fair. Not only was she leaving the Harvey Company without an answer, but her mother, as well. "I'll let you know soon. I promise."

"As long as we know by spring." Mother smiled across the mule's back at her betrothed. "We've set the wedding date for then."

"That's wonderful. I'm—" Sean sidled up to her, halting the conversation.

"What a pleasant surprise," he said. "We can get to know each other better." His gaze flicked to her outfit. "Is that a split leather skirt?" His eyes widened.

"Yes, it is." She lifted her chin. "Much more practical with sharp thorns than cotton."

"Hmm." He shrugged. "Ride in front of me so I can keep an eye on you."

"How about you ride in front of me?" She crossed her arms.

"McMurray has a point," Dallas interjected. "I'd like

you and Mrs. Rollins in the middle. I'm tour guide and my rules are nonnegotiable. Also, crowd the rock face as much as possible. Don't worry about Hero, he's been well-trained and the mules are used to him. If you feel your mount is having trouble negotiating the trail, give me a holler. Everyone in the saddle! We're off to a late start."

Because of her, he might as well have added. Putting her left foot in the stirrup, Annie swung into the saddle. She could barely control her glee as they headed over the canyon edge and down the trail. Her heart skipped, and she wanted to laugh out loud. If she were alone, she would have. For now, she'd be content with a grin that hurt her cheeks.

The scenery took her breath away. While stunning from the top, the beauty of the canyon only increased farther down. The line of mules appeared to be nothing more than ants in the great expanse.

Annie wished she was a painter so she could capture the scene in an artistic form. A bird with a wingspan larger than the mules were long soared on an air current. "What is that?"

"A condor," Dallas called back. "That is a rare sight indeed."

The majestic bird, with its pink bald head and inky feathers, dipped and dived, until finally disappearing like a bullet from a gun. Annie craned her neck to try and see where it had gone.

"They perch on the cliff face." Dallas glanced over his shoulder, tossing her a smile. "You'll see many beautiful sights today."

His hat cast his face in shadow. His white teeth flashed from his tanned face. Annie caught her breath, realizing she might not see anything in the canyon as magnificent as Dallas Baker.

*

The canyon was deep in shadow by the time they stopped and pitched their tents. Dallas hated heading out late. Now, he'd have to fix a simple meal of eggs and bacon for supper. He supposed flapjacks would do for breakfast.

"I'll handle the food if you help my daughter pitch our tent." Mrs. Rollins took the cast-iron skillet from him. "She isn't as self-sufficient as she thinks she is."

Dallas glanced to where Annie fought to pitch a tent that seemed bent on collapsing on her head. "I'll help her and gladly hand over cooking duties."

Before Dallas could get to Annie's side, McMurray stepped in. Dallas sighed and chose instead to see if any of the others needed help. They didn't, not being first-timers. For once, Dallas had little to do. He could take the dog and scout out a fishing spot for the next day, but since they always camped in the same place, that seemed like a waste of time.

He grinned and shoved his hat farther back on his head. "Come on, Hero. Let's walk."

The rush of river water, the rustle of brush as small rodents hid, and the twinkling of stars as they blinked against a velvet sky made the evening perfect. Almost. Annie's laugh drifted his way. He would've loved to be able to walk hand in hand with her and point out the things she'd never seen.

But they'd been nothing more than passing strangers, at best acquaintances, over the last few months. Several times Dallas had almost approached her, ready to spill his guts about his feelings toward her, but then she'd say something about renewing her Harvey contract. That wouldn't work for Dallas. He'd already made up his mind to return to Texas in the spring.

Being around Annie, hearing her laugh, seeing her face, were all too much for him. He'd broken things off with Dottie back in July, and she'd requested to be transferred. Since then, Dallas had kept his distance from women.

He smiled. Annie and her split skirts, this new one leather, with fringe, tended to make him smile rather than frown nowadays. What would she come up with next? He had to admit he liked her in the new ensemble, with her hair falling down her back in a single, thick, golden braid, and a worn leather hat too big for her head. Her father's, he'd guess. The trail was the perfect place for split skirts, and he was wise enough to see the reasoning.

Ma was right. Dallas tended to judge folks for being themselves. Annie was every bit the lady when she needed to be, and strong enough to get her hands dirty when the need arose. He bent and searched the ground for a rock, then flicked his wrist, sending it skittering across the water. Too dark to count the skips, he took to throwing and listening to the plunks.

Mrs. Rollins called out that supper was ready. Dallas whistled for Hero and stalked back to the camp. "Smells good." He accepted the tin bowl she handed him, and glanced appreciatively at a rich stew. "Maybe we should hire you as permanent cook on these tours."

"No, I'll soon be cooking for only one man." She smiled at Mr. Harris. "We've decided to move to his home state."

"Where's that?" Dallas sat and leaned against a

boulder.

"I'm from Dallas, Texas, son." Mr. Harris sat across the fire from him. "Not too far from your folks, I reckon."

"Texas is a big state," Annie insisted.

He shook his head. "Everyone in Texas is a neighbor."

Dallas agreed. Texans knew no strangers. He wished he could see Annie's face. What did she think of her mother, Dallas, all moving away without her? Maybe Mrs. Rollins could talk Annie into accepting a Harvey position at one of the stations in Texas. Then she'd be close to her family…and to him.

"I'm not hungry." Annie set her bowl on the rocks circling the fire. "I'm turning in." She rushed to the tent.

"I suppose I should've told her in private first." Mrs. Rollins turned her head toward the tent. "But we only decided last night."

Mr. Harris patted her hand. "Give her time, then talk to her. In the morning, perhaps. She'll understand."

"So, you'll be selling the house?" Dallas ladled more stew into his bowl.

"Most likely, if Annie doesn't want it." Mrs. Rollins sighed. "It was more my late husband's house then mine. I wanted to stay back East, not provide room and board to strangers. But it did provide a living after his death. I won't belittle him about the decision."

Dallas's spirit fell. Without a house, Annie would surely leave Arizona. He couldn't fault her. He had his own plans to return home. The problem was, he didn't know how he could handle not knowing where she was. If she kept the house, even if he didn't see her all the time, at least he'd know that.

McMurray straightened his shoulders. "I may have a proposition for Annie that will solve everyone's problems." He looked around the circle. "Pastor Carson is moving to California. I've decided to take his place as pastor here."

Good for the townsfolk, but Dallas wasn't so sure about Annie. Maybe she cared more about the young pastor than he knew. Well, if so, he wouldn't stand in the way of her happiness. He'd keep his mouth shut and see how things played out. He had several months before spring. Months of cold winter to see exactly what Annie's plans were.

Maybe, if God was so inclined, Dallas could find a way to mend the rift between him and Annie. Anything could happen in six months.

19

Annie banged the skillet against the rocks. She'd burned the biscuits. What had possessed her to believe she could cook over a campfire? This was nothing like the stove at home. With a groan, she tossed the toasty lumps of hard dough into the bushes.

"You shouldn't throw away food," Dallas said, snapping his suspenders over a faded undershirt. "It attracts wild animals."

She straightened. "Really? They'd come close? Oh, I'd love to see something."

He laughed. "There are certain animals up here you'd rather not see close up, believe me." He took the pan from her. "I'll mix up flapjacks. They're easier. Want me to show you how?"

"Sure." She sighed and sat back on her haunches. First, he'd laughed at her attempts to set up a tent, now he thought her mishap at cooking hilarious and pitiful.

If he laughed at her one more time...

"Good morning." Mother emerged from the tent, shoving a hairpin into her bun. "What a brisk morning."

"Another couple of weeks and it'll be more than brisk," Dallas said, pouring batter into a pan. "It'll be downright cold."

Annie leaned forward to get a better look at the way the pancakes bubbled around the corners. Not so different from the stove. Why had she had trouble? Ah. She'd set the pan smack-dab in the middle of the fire, while Dallas had it off to one side and continuously moved it. What could she make for supper that would show him she wasn't a complete idiot?

"Sleep well?"

"Fair." She'd tossed and turned all night. Rocks poked her hips and back. She'd wondered what the attraction of camping was. So far, the experience left something to be desired.

"There's a great spot for fishing down the river, if anyone's interested." Dallas slid a flapjack onto a plate and handed it to Annie.

"Thank you. Yes, that might be fun." Although she'd never baited her own hook. Father had always taken care of that for her. She tossed Hero a small bite of her breakfast. How hard could it be to thread a worm onto a hook? She was starting to think she didn't know as much about surviving in the outdoors as she'd let herself believe.

No wonder Mother had hired a guide. She had more sense than her daughter. Annie could not in any way have led a tour into the canyon.

Spending her childhood in the boardinghouse, and the occasional afternoon fishing, had not prepared her for the roughness of the wilderness. Well, she was smart and able. She could learn.

She studied Dallas's strong face. He had no trouble adapting to the great outdoors. Rather, he seemed to thrive. Always confident, he appeared completely at home hunkered over a fire, serving breakfast. As confident as he did brushing his horse or saving an endangered child. Did she have as many interesting aspects?

If the way Sean's gaze constantly fell on her was any indication, she did, but she certainly didn't feel it. Rather boring was how she would describe herself. She cut another glance at Dallas and caught him watching her.

He stared without turning away, capturing her gaze like a fish on a hook. Everyone else seemed to disappear. After an eternity, the corner of his mouth quirked and he lowered his eyes. "Food all right?"

"Delicious." She forced out the word, her voice hoarse.

"You aren't growing ill from the chill last night, are you?" Sean peered into her face. "You look flushed."

"I'm fine. The fire's a bit warm, is all." She set her plate on a boulder and got to her feet. Avoiding her mother's gaze, she ducked out of sight into her tent, clasping a hand over her rapidly beating heart.

What had she seen in Dallas's eyes? Admiration? Affection? Dare she hope he had growing feelings for her? Feelings he managed to shutter whenever Sean was around?

Foolish girl. Dallas wasn't a man to hold back for anyone, much less a mild-mannered gentleman like Sean. No, most likely Dallas stared at her as if she were a species he'd never seen. She only imagined the soft look in his eyes.

After shoving her feet into an old pair of boots she had used for mucking out the barn before Dallas arrived, she headed back to the others and collected the now empty dishes. She carried them to the riverbank and scoured them clean with a handful of coarse sand.

An eagle screeched overhead, then dived to the water's surface, rising again with a fish in its long claws. Annie could sit and watch the scenery for hours. There was so much more to see down there than from the top. If only it didn't take a day to reach the bottom and another to get back to the top. She'd make sure to soak in as much of the experience as possible. Then, when she gazed at the canyon from the top, she could fill in the blank spots from memory.

When she returned to the campsite, Dallas had already passed out fishing poles. "I saved one for you."

"Thank you." This she knew how to do.

"The spot I'm taking y'all to is perfect for bank fishing or fly angling. If you don't mind getting wet, I suggest the latter."

Annie wanted to ask what angling was, but since she knew how to fish from the bank, she'd stick to that and not show her ignorance. She couldn't stand any more teasing.

"I managed to catch some live bait this morning for the bank fishers," he said.

"That would be me." Annie held her hand out for the bucket. Why was there water in the worms? She peered inside. "I'm using fish to catch fish? How am I supposed to get them on the hook?"

"Hook them under the spine." Dallas grinned.

"Nothing better than live bait for this river."

Her shoulders slumped. What she wouldn't give for a big fat worm.

*

Dallas grinned, remembering the look on Annie's face when he'd handed her the pail of small fish. He admired her grit and determination. Only a blind man couldn't see how hard she tried to act as if camping wasn't a new experience for her. What would she have done if she'd actually succeeded in convincing her mother to let her guide people? He shook his head. What a disaster that would've been for everyone involved.

He whistled for Hero to follow, chuckling as the six-month-old pup bounded over low bushes. Young or not, the dog would be a good warning if a dangerous critter ventured close, which Dallas doubted would happen. Not with a crowd of adults, anyway. A single person might be a different story.

He led the group to his favorite fishing spot and had them spread out along the bank. He positioned Annie on the edge of a rock that jutted over the water. "It isn't too swift here if you fall in, and the fish are usually biting. Do you want me to bait your hook?"

"No, thank you." She scowled and plunged her hand into the bucket. "Slippery little things." She finally grasped one and grimaced, clutching it in her fist. "See?" The fish squirmed, wiggling free of her grasp and falling into the river.

Dallas laughed. "Let me help you before you lose them all."

"There's plenty." She reached for another one. "Go away."

"Are you sure you don't want me to teach you to angle?"

"I'm positive." She straightened and planted her fists on her hips. "Now, if you're finished ridiculing me, I'd like to catch a fish."

He back away, hands raised. "Holler if you need me."

"I doubt that will happen," she muttered. Tongue between her teeth, she struggled to pierce the slippery fish with her hook.

Dallas laughed again and went to check on the others. Annie sure was cute when riled.

Fly angling would have given him the opportunity to put his arms around her while teaching her how to cast the line over the water, back and forth, back and forth, flicking her delicate wrist just so. He would've enjoyed that. Gathering her close on the pretense of teaching her a new way to fish. He glanced over his shoulder and sighed at the sight of McMurray making his way to her side.

She'd probably relent and let him help her. For a reason Dallas couldn't fathom, Annie didn't want to accept any assistance from him. Almost as if she needed to prove herself. That was his fault, most likely. Him and his former prejudiced ways.

What if she never forgave him? What if he returned to Texas not having set things right between them? Ma would have his hide for sure.

A shout drew his attention back to Annie. She tugged at her pole, yanking it up and down like a water pump.

"Don't lose it." Dallas leaped across the rocks to try and reach her.

She glanced his way, lost her footing on the slippery boulder and tumbled into the river.

His heart lodged in his throat. What if the water was deeper than he'd thought? Her leather skirt could weigh her down. He waited for her head to appear, and watched in horror as she appeared farther downstream, caught in an undercurrent.

With no further thought, he leaped in after her. "Hold on!"

He stayed close to the bank and swam as hard as he could, letting the current carry him toward Annie. She grabbed a low-hanging branch and hugged it, wrapping both arms and legs around the limb. Smart girl.

Dallas reached her, planting his booted feet firmly on the river's bottom. "Put your arms around my neck. I'll carry you on my back."

"No." Her eyes widened. "That isn't proper at all."

"You're wearing a split skirt. It's no different than pants, isn't that what you say?" Now was not the time for propriety.

She laced her arms around his neck. "I'm ready."

He was holding her, albeit not in the way he'd originally planned. Holding her legs tight around his middle, he sloshed through the water to the bank, then turned her over to the care of her mother. "She'd best get into some dry clothes."

Mrs. Rollins nodded. "Come along, daughter. You, too, Mr. Baker."

"I'm fine. One of the others might need assistance."

She narrowed her eyes. "You may return after you are dry." Taking her daughter's arm, she marched back to camp. "Annie, while you change your clothes, I'll get a fire going," Esther said.

Annie nodded and retreated to her tent, while Dallas ducked into his. The thought of what might have happened had he not been close chilled him more than the water. The river wasn't deep in that spot, but with a skirt, and panicked, Annie might not have made it out.

He quickly changed his clothes, putting back on his wet boots. He wouldn't chance ruining his better pair. The dry socks would have to be enough. When he emerged, Mrs. Rollins was stirring the fire's embers.

Rustling inside the tent told him Annie was still changing. He averted his head and made his way quickly back to the others, not wanting to dwell on what she might be taking off in the privacy there.

"Annie all right?" McMurray rushed to meet him. "Should I check on her?"

"Her mother is with her. She'll be fine." Dallas shouldn't have stopped the man from going, but McMurray wasn't the one who'd jumped to her rescue. He'd stood on the bank and watched helplessly while she'd been swept downstream.

"I feel awful," the other man said, staring across the river. "But I can't swim a lick. Have a horrible fear of the water. Not seemly for a man of God to fear something, is it?"

"Sounds healthy to me." Dallas continued walking, making the man follow if he wanted to continue the conversation.

"Maybe so." McMurray sighed. "You're a regular saver of mankind, Mr. Baker. Completely deserving of the title hero the townspeople have labeled you."

Dallas stopped and stared at the man. He just did what needed doing. Nothing heroic about his actions. "But you, Pastor, are a saver of souls." And seemed to have captured the heart of the woman Dallas loved.

20

Annie wanted nothing more to do with the camping trip. Instead, she wanted to head home and renew her contract with the Harvey Company. Then there'd be no more being laughed at, no more feeling as if she were keeping her mother from her own future, no more worry about what came next in Annie's life.

The moment her mother rejoined Mr. Harris fishing, Annie stuffed her saddlebags, filled her canteen and then saddled her mule. She needed to be moving up the trail before anyone caught wind of what she planned.

She couldn't think about the irresponsibility of what she was doing. After all, what danger could there be? All she had to do was the follow the trail back to the top. The mule probably knew the way. He'd traversed it enough times over the summer. Once they got on the trail, there would be nowhere to go but up.

Yanking on the lead rope, Annie set off in the

direction they'd hiked the day before. If she followed the river in the opposite direction from camp, she'd be bound to find the trail. She scanned the cliff face. Why couldn't she see it? Was the entrance hidden behind the thick brush?

With the river on her left and the cliff on her right, she had only three directions in which to go: forward, backward, or up, which was the one she preferred, if she could only find the trail. She discarded the middle option.

The sun was high in the sky by the time she stopped for a drink in front of a mound of what looked like fallen boulders. She dug in her saddlebags for a piece of dried meat and hard biscuit. While she ate, she watched an eagle soar overhead. Maybe she'd catch another rare glimpse of a condor.

The shade felt cool on her heated shoulders, and she leaned against the rocks to take a break. If she'd ridden the mule, she wouldn't be so tired, but she wanted the animal rested when it was time to start the climb.

Except Annie now knew without a doubt that she was lost. Tears stung her eyes. She'd have to swallow her pride and follow the river back to camp. She reached for the mule's lead. "Come on, animal. Let's head back." She would never hear the end of the ridicule.

The mule tossed its head, yanking the rope from her hands. It released a loud bray and galloped away.

"What in the world? Get back here!" Annie stomped her foot. What could possibly—

A scream sounded over her shoulder. Spiders with icy feet crawled up her spine. She'd heard that sound before from the safety of her special place overlooking the canyon. As slowly as possible, she turned.

A cougar stared down at her from what could only be its lair. Two smaller heads poked up from the rocks.

Annie's heart stopped. Her breath caught. What should she do now? She'd stumbled upon a mama who would do anything to protect her young. The animal had no idea that Annie wouldn't hurt her babies.

Searching the ground for a weapon, she settled on a stick as thick as her wrist. Still moving slowly, she removed her knife from her belt and took a step backward. Father always said not to run when facing a wild animal To make yourself as large as possible so they'd think it more trouble to attack you than it was worth. Hard to do when everything in her wanted to flee as fast as possible.

When the animal continued to watch her with its beautiful golden eyes, Annie took another step. She held the stick and knife over her head and prayed for God to release her from her foolishness. Oh, my. What if His answer to that prayer was death at the teeth of a wildcat? She quickly amended her prayer to include a safe return home for her and the animal.

Not that she thought God too stupid to decipher the true meaning of her prayer…but she was rambling. Her mouth filled with cotton. Every time her foot sent a rock clattering against another, an icy stream of perspiration ran down her back.

She peered over her shoulder at the rushing river. Why couldn't she have stopped to rest at a calm location? She'd drown if she were to try and cross. But then again, the cat wouldn't follow her. She shook her head. No, she'd continue on this side of the river, one tiny step at a time.

With each step she took, the cat took one, too. Its

deep-throated growls made Annie's knees weak. *Don't fall. Don't fall.* Stupid mule, leaving her alone.

Her hand started to sweat around the handle of her knife. She tightened her grip. To lose her weapons meant certain death. *Oh, please, go away.* She couldn't win against an animal that weighed more than she did. All she could hope for was to hurt it enough to make it want to go away instead of eat her.

She wiped her teary eyes on her sleeve. Couldn't animals sense weakness? Smell her fear? How did one face such a situation and not be afraid?

She wanted to cry, scream, call out for Dallas. *God, please send help.*

*

Dallas leaned his pole against a rock. A saddled mule chewed a patch of dry grass beside the tents. Dallas glanced toward the makeshift paddock and counted the animals there. One was missing. "Mrs. Rollins, did Annie say anything about taking a ride?"

"No, only that she wanted to rest." She parted the tent flaps. "She's gone. So are her bags." She backed out. "Where could she have gone without a mule?"

Dallas's thoughts, exactly. Fear took root in his stomach and spread tendrils through his limbs. Had she been thrown? Did she lie injured and dying beside the trail? He whistled for Hero and sprinted for Rascal.

Within fifteen minutes, he was riding toward the trail and watching for signs of someone having recently passed that way. Why wasn't he seeing any? Was it possible she'd gotten lost and headed in the wrong direction?

He stopped and listened. Waited for direction from God to show him the way. A strong urge to follow the river tugged at him. He steered his horse away from the trail. Ma had taught him a long time ago that sometimes God's direction came in a gentle nudging. Other times, in a fierce scream. Dallas had learned not to ignore either one.

There. A hoofprint. A strike of a steel shoe against a rock. Unless there was another party down here, he'd found the direction Annie had wandered.

The scream of a mountain cat froze Dallas's blood. That sound meant only one thing: the cat felt threatened. Annie! He spurred Rascal faster, despite the horse's reluctance to move. Hero set up a shrill barking from between the horse's legs. Dallas needed to dismount before someone was hurt.

He slid from the saddle and tethered his horse to a low bush, then slipped his rifle from its scabbard. "Hush, Hero. Down boy."

"Dallas!" Annie's cry spurred him into a run.

He burst around the curve and skidded to a halt. She stood like a warrior, hair falling around her shoulders in a glorious wave of gold, a club in one hand and a knife in the other. He didn't think he'd ever seen a more magnificent, or scary, sight in his life. "Get behind me."

"I can't. My foot is stuck and I can't pull out of my boot. Help me." She raised wide eyes and a tear-streaked face toward him.

Dallas planted himself in front of her. "Stay, Hero." The pup took up a stance beside him and barked. The sound echoed off the canyon walls. Dallas aimed his rifle, hoping he wouldn't have to shoot. He didn't want to kill a mother.

"I can't see." Annie shoved against him. "Stand beside me. There's strength in numbers, even in the animal kingdom. My father taught me that."

He took two steps to the side, wanting to protect her, love her, not put her in danger because she wanted to feel independent. But now was not the time to argue. He fired a shot into the air.

The cat stared him down, giving another roar.

He fired again.

With a growl, the cougar pulled back out of sight. There was not time to waste. She could return, and Dallas needed to get Annie to safety. "Hold this." He handed her the rifle and knelt to remove the large rocks that had fallen on her foot. "Does anything feel broken?"

"No." She juggled the gun and her stick. "My boot protected the bones, but I couldn't pull free. I would've been too exposed if I stooped to unlace it."

The moment she was free, Dallas cupped her face. "You sure you're all right?" He could've lost her. The thought sent his heart to his toes. What if he'd never seen her again? Never had the opportunity to tell her he loved her?

"I'm fine. Thank you for—"

"Annie!" McMurray and the other men raced toward them.

She stepped back, leaving Dallas feeling more alone than he'd ever felt in his life. He took his rifle from her and kept an eye on the cougar's den. Not that he expected the animal to reappear, not with a crowd of people there.

McMurray pulled Annie into his arms. She stiffened, giving Dallas a bit of hope that she didn't completely return the other man's feelings. Maybe she didn't like public displays of affection, and that was why she didn't return his embrace? His shoulders slumped.

"We'd best get back," he said. "It'll be dark soon." He led the way, retrieving Rascal from where he'd tethered him. The last thing he wanted to do was stay and watch McMurray gush over Annie.

Dallas's heart couldn't take it. He gave God thanks for her safety as he led the others back to camp, and also gave thanks that they'd be returning home in the morning. Spring wouldn't come soon enough. Suddenly, Dallas wanted to go home to Texas, although he knew he'd leave part of his heart in Arizona with a yellow-haired gal.

But northern Arizona winters would keep them cooped up inside and thrust into each other's company. Anything could happen. Maybe, by warmer weather, Dallas would have won Annie's heart. His steps lighter, he unsaddled Rascal.

Mrs. Rollins hefted her skirts and ran to her daughter, gathering her in her arms. "Oh, my dear, I thought we'd lost you." She caressed Annie's face. "What possessed you to leave us?"

Annie's shoulders slumped and she glanced toward Dallas. "I just wanted to go home."

Had he done something to cause her to run off? He set the saddle on the ground and searched his mind. He'd rescued her from the river. Surely that hadn't angered her. What could he have said to hurt her feelings?

He marched to where she sat nursing a cup of coffee. "May I speak to you, please?"

Her face paled, but she nodded before following him to where the animals were tethered. "Yes?"

"What caused you to leave, Annie?" He reached out

to touch her, then thought better of it and pulled his hand away. "Did I say or do something to cause you pain?"

She closed her eyes and ducked her head. "I realized how inadequate I was at camping or fishing. I didn't sleep well the night before because of the hard ground—"

"Did you sweep away the rocks?"

She met his gaze with a glare. "See? That's my point. I couldn't even think of something so simple to make myself more comfortable. I'm not cut out for this kind of life, vacation or not."

He gripped her shoulders and grinned. "You're perfect for this. Annie, love, you single-handedly stared down a mountain lion."

21

"I'd like to renew my contract through March." Annie stood before Miss Cartwright, her hands folded in front of her. "There's little enough to do in the winter, and I can use the money."

The head waitress laughed. "I've heard of worse reasons for a girl to renew. I'm glad to have you back."

Annie forced a smile. Since their return from the canyon tour a week ago, Dallas had avoided her like the plague, Mother was wrapped up in Mr. Harris and Annie felt very much alone.

At first, Mother had spent a couple days doting and fussing over Annie, then it was back to business as usual. Except there was no business. Any tourists arriving at the Grand Canyon during the cold winter tended to book rooms at El Tovar. While Mother continued to bake for the hotel, she seemed to care little about whether she had boarders or not.

Her waning enthusiasm for the business was the final straw in Annie's decision to renew her contract. Come spring, she'd help her mother sell the house, then she'd follow the railroad. Maybe to California. She'd heard the weather was mild and the ocean fantastic.

"I can begin right away. As soon as I put on my uniform." Annie headed to the seamstress, sure the woman still had the one tailored to fit her. There weren't many women as tall as she was.

Once dressed, she entered the dining room, pleased that Miss Cartwright had reinstated her at her current position, and searched for Dallas. Her spirits drooped when she didn't see him.

He'd called her love, then walked away. Confusion clouded her mind. Maybe the endearment was a slip of the tongue. She'd read too much meaning into the simple word. Even retiring her split skirt to her bedroom trunk hadn't elicited more attention from Dallas. No, the only man who came calling was Sean. Annie felt as if Mother was already planning her wedding.

Annie shrugged. If she was married, Mother could leave with Mr. Harris without worrying about her.

After collecting the drink pitchers, Annie rolled the cart to the waiting customers, pasted on a smile and got to work. Maybe she *would* focus on becoming a head waitress. It was a respected position, after all. She could have her pick of restaurants across the country.

Her gaze fell on the eager face of Sean. Of course, there was the matter of one Pastor McMurray. She'd taken to sitting in the front row while he preached every Sunday. Folks seemed to expect it, even going so far as to hint about them having a courtship. Annie would sit in the back row this week. Hopefully, Sean would get the hint without her having to voice the words.

While he was an extremely kind man, handsome and well-mannered, Annie didn't love him as a woman should love the man she married. Her heart belonged to a man who seemed to only tolerate her. It promised to be a long winter.

"Miss?" A woman held up her coffee mug. "Are you going to pour?"

Annie's face heated. She'd stood lost in her thoughts long enough for a customer to notice.

Miss Cartwright frowned from across the room. If Annie kept getting distracted, the head waitress might regret signing her on again, and demote her back to the lunch counter. Annie had a job to do, so she'd best do it and do it well. Moping would get her nowhere.

Besides, she wasn't one to let life pass her by. She'd always forged ahead to experience it at its fullest. Why should now be any different? So things didn't go as planned. She'd shake it off and continue. God had bigger and better things in store for her.

Better than Dallas? Her hands shook. She'd like to think so, but had a hard time wrapping her mind around it. Perhaps God didn't intend her to marry, and she should stop fretting. She would experience what life had to offer and if God wanted her to wed, then He would prepare the way.

She'd been perfectly content to seek out life's experiences until Dallas strolled into the boardinghouse that day. Shortly after, her world had been turned upside down and her heart wrung out. Since the first glimpse of his face, her life hadn't been the same.

She grinned, knowing she wouldn't have changed any of it. Sure, her heart might ache at knowing he wasn't hers, but not knowing him would've been worse. She gave thanks to God for the precious friendship they'd shared. She'd seek Dallas out at the first opportunity and let him know how much he meant to her. As a friend. She didn't want to make him uncomfortable, after all.

With her mood lightened after realizing that she could have a relationship with Dallas without it having to be a romantic one, she floated through her day. She performed her duties almost without thinking, and ended the day satisfied and fulfilled.

After work, she headed to the barn. Light spilled from its open doors. She stood in the doorway and watched as Dallas cleaned his horse's feet. He'd removed his coat in the warmth of the barn, and his muscles rippled under the cotton of his shirt. It might be harder than she'd thought to look at him as only a friend, but God had given Annie an inner strength. She could rely on it in a time such as this.

"Dallas?" She pleated her apron, anxious that he might take her words wrong and not accept friendship at all.

"Good evening, Annie." He straightened. "Is everything all right?"

"Very." She drew a deep breath. "I haven't properly thanked you for rescuing me from the cougar. I couldn't help but notice how you've...avoided me since. And, well, I value—"

*

"Value what?" It took all of Dallas's willpower not to throw the pick he used to dig stones out of Rascal's shoes. Annie had to be the most infuriating female he'd ever met.

"Why, our friendship, of course."

He shook his head, wanting to shake some sense into her. Why couldn't she see he wanted to be more than friends? Well, if that's the way she wanted it, then that's what they'd be. Friends. He huffed. "So do I."

"You sound facetious." She tilted her head to the side.

Turning away before she could discern his true feelings, he shrugged. "Nope. Not a bit."

What a liar. He sighed and started brushing Rascal's coat. The horse picked up on his mood and grew restless, snorting and stomping his feet. "Hush, boy."

"I understand." She turned to leave.

"Understand what, Annie?" Dallas stilled his brushing and stared at her over the horse's back. "What exactly do you understand?"

"You have no desire to be friends." She squared her shoulders. "And I respect your decision. But since we are living in such close quarters, and winter is upon us, we should at least be civil with each other, don't you agree?"

He closed his eyes and rested his forehead on Rascal's shoulder. "Yes, I agree." Frustrated, he said nothing to prevent her from walking away. He needed time to form his thoughts into words before saying something he'd regret.

The two of them needed to stop dancing around each other and speak plainly. At least he did. If Ma knew he had yet to tell Annie he loved her, she'd skin him alive. If he were a betting man, he'd wager Rascal's saddle that Ma expected him to show up at the ranch with Annie come spring.

By the time he had Rascal curried, smells of supper were drifting across the yard. Sometimes it was hard telling his stomach to wait until Annie got home to eat, but he understood Mrs. Rollins's reasoning.

He stomped the mud off his boots and entered through the back door, Hero on his heels. After washing up in the mud room, he continued toward the dining room. Mr. Harris's booming laugh echoed, followed by Mrs. Rollins's giggle, and another man's answering laugh. Dallas wanted to kick something. McMurray must have been invited to supper.

"Feel free to take a bite out of his leg," he told the dog. "It'll be dark under the table. Hard for a mutt to see, right?" He scratched Hero behind the ears, glad he'd been allowed access to the house after proving how well behaved he was, and then marched to the table. "Food smells good. Evening, McMurray." He might as well be mannerly. The sight of a roasted chicken, bowls of mashed potatoes and green beans, and a basket of biscuits made his stomach rumble. Mrs. Rollins sure did know how to cook.

"Good evening, Mr. Baker. We were just getting

ready to say the blessing."

Avoiding Annie's eyes, Dallas took a seat as far from her as the small kitchen table would allow. Why was it that every time he built up the nerve to tell her of his love, McMurray showed up?

Dallas could hear his mother's voice ringing in his ears, saying, *"When did you become such a coward, son?"* He sighed and laid his napkin across his lap.

"Although I was a bit put out at first that our dear Annie renewed her contract with the Harvey Company," McMurray said, spearing a biscuit with his fork, "I understand a woman's need to keep occupied."

What did he miss? The entire blessing? And now McMurray was rattling on about Annie. Dallas needed to pay closer attention instead of losing himself in his head.

"Please don't speak for me," Annie said, her brows drawing together. "I renewed my contract so I could travel down the rail line come spring."

Sean's eyes widened. "You've already decided to renew again? Annie, the winter is long and you may change—"

"I won't change my mind, Sean." She set her fork beside her plate, lining it up perfectly with the plate's edge. "I've never kept it a secret from you that I have no plans to marry."

"But..." He expelled a sharp breath, his lips fluttering. "Mrs. Rollins, surely you—"

"The supper table is no place to discuss this," Mrs. Rollins admonished. "This is a private matter between the two of you. While I have my own hopes for my daughter, I will not push her into anything she does not desire."

Dallas switched his gaze from one to the other. When his gaze met Mr. Harris's, the older man shrugged and refocused on his food.

Annie had no feelings for McMurray? The knowledge warmed Dallas more than the food. If she spurned the other man's courtship, Dallas had ample opportunity to win her heart during the winter. He could bide his time instead of rushing to tell her of his love.

He lifted a chicken leg to his mouth. Unless another gentleman entered the picture. One who could offer Annie the adventure she craved.

Would being a rancher's wife provide enough excitement for her? Ma seemed content, but maybe that wasn't the life for every woman. Ranching was hard work. There was planting, calving, round-up, branding…the work never ended. Why, a family rarely left the ranch unless there was a big to-do in town.

He focused on Annie's beautiful face. The thought that ranching, that he, might not be enough for her, chilled his heart.

"Are you going to eat that chicken leg or keep smelling it?" Annie gave him a wry grin.

Dallas stared at the meat in his hand. What in tarnation was wrong with him? He was acting like a schoolboy with a crush.

"I'm thinking the lad has a woman on his mind," Mr. Harris said. "When a man is in love, he can't focus on anything else."

Annie's eyes widened and her mouth opened.

Dallas couldn't pull his gaze away.

22

"Playing with you is no fun." Annie sat back and crossed her arms, glaring at the checkerboard. "I'm no competition for you."

"But you make a pretty picture sitting across the table." Dallas winked and jumped another of her pieces.

He'd been nothing but attentive, offering flattery at every turn, since she'd finally managed to convince Sean there could be nothing between them. That was four months ago, and Dallas still hadn't said a word about love. She almost felt as if he treated her like a younger sister, except for the look of admiration in his eyes.

If he didn't make his feelings clear soon, she'd have to step over the boundaries of propriety and take the initiative. That might be wickedly delightful.

"What are you grinning about?" Dallas claimed another of her pieces. "You're losing badly."

She laughed. "You have no idea who the loser will be, Dallas Baker. No idea at all."

He frowned and stared at her. "Are you tired?" He glanced at the mantel. "It's only eight o'clock, but you've been putting in long hours at the hotel, and—"

"I'm fine. Really." She stifled another smile and studied the board. He had one more move and it would be game over. In life as well as checkers.

Annie would give him until it was time to renew her contract in two months. If he didn't say anything by then, she'd tell him how she felt and say goodbye. Renewing her contract didn't mean she had to stay at El Tovar. She glanced around the room. She sure would miss the old house and the view of the canyon. Maybe she could visit home once in a while if they sent her away. She doubted the Harvey Company would let her stay at El Tovar indefinitely.

"Do you want me to put the game away?" Dallas asked.

"No, I'll do it. I'm not heading to bed right away." She stood and swept the pieces into their wood box. "Good night, Dallas."

He stood. Moving close, he ran his thumb along her jaw, sending prickles along her arms and stealing her breath. "Good night, Annette Rollins."

When he left without giving her the kiss she yearned for, she slapped the checkerboard in half and added it to the box. She was deluding herself. The man gave her tender touches and kind glances, but never went so far as to hold her hand. Ugh, he frustrated her so.

"Shouldn't you be headed to bed, dear?" Mother turned down the wick on one of the lanterns. "You have work in the morning."

"May I ask you a question?"

Mother turned. "Of course." She motioned to the settee. "Should we sit or move to the kitchen for tea?"

"Tea would be nice. I'll finish up in here and join you in a few minutes." Annie set the game box on the fireplace mantel and extinguished the last lamp. She rarely asked her mother for advice, but the situation with Dallas warranted it. She could tell from the occasional looks on her mother's face that she often wondered what was going on between her daughter and their tour guide.

With the parlor put to rights, Annie joined her n the kitchen, where water boiled on the stove and fine china teacups were set on matching saucers. Annie smiled. Since Mother had found love, her stern demeanor had softened, making her the woman Annie remembered from before her father's death.

"Now." Mother sat at the table. "Tell me what's on your mind."

Annie pulled out a chair. "I'm not sure how to begin but...how do you get a man to express himself? I mean, you and Mr. Harris have been courting for months. Why are you waiting so long to get married?"

Mother smiled. "You're asking about two different things. Let's start with Mr. Harris." She tapped her chin with her forefinger. "I loved your father, dearly, you know that, but things weren't always rosy with us. For one, I did not relish being uprooted from my home and brought here. He let me have very little say in the matter. I'm afraid that after his death, I may have been too forward in my opinions to make up for that.

"So, before I hitch my wagon to another man, so to speak, I intend to be sure that we want the same things out of life."

Annie nodded. "Such as the freedom to travel."

"Exactly. We aren't getting any younger, and now that you're grown, there is nothing to tie me here." She waved off Annie's protest. "Of course, I'll miss you, but I'll have the freedom to visit you anytime I can get a train ticket."

The teakettle whistled and Mother leaped up to take it from the stove. "As for getting a man to speak about his feelings, why, dear, that's been an ongoing battle for women since the dawn of time. Are we talking about Dallas?"

"Yes." Annie sighed. "Sometimes he looks at me as a man looks at a woman he cares about, and at other times he treats me like a younger sister. Spring is almost here. I'd like to know how he feels about me."

Mother glanced over her shoulder. "You love him?"

"Very much, and it terrifies me to think he may not feel the same."

"Oh, he feels the same way." Mother set the teapot in front of her. "It's written on his face. He's scared out of his wits."

Annie nodded. "I'm giving him until the end of my current contract to say something. If not, I'll tell him I love him and I'll leave. He can follow me or not."

"I'm sorry you're going through this turmoil." Mother reached out and pressed her hand.

Annie was afraid to move. Her mother rarely showed her any open affection, other than a smothering hug after the cougar incident. Annie put her free hand over hers and squeezed back.

"I may need your help picking up the poor man off the ground when I tell him I love him."

*

Dallas lay in bed and stared at the ceiling. Why didn't he kiss Annie? He'd had the perfect opportunity. Her sweet lips had been lifted to his, her face soft under his touch. It took all his inner strength to take things slowly. For him to woo her as one would a wild horse. Not that Annie was a horse. Not at all. More like a deer.

He had two more months to make her love him. Oh, she was beginning to; he saw it in her eyes. Maybe there was more there than he thought. He'd had so little experience with females. The isolation of the ranch had left little time for mingling with the fairer gender. He should have asked more questions of Ma and Pa while growing up. Even his brothers knew more than he did, especially since one of them was married.

Dallas rolled over and punched his pillow. He sure had lost a lot of sleep thinking about Annie over the months he'd lived in Arizona. Wouldn't his brothers get a kick out of his haggard face?

Spring would arrive soon, and Dallas felt a lurch in his spirit at the thought of leaving the Grand Canyon. It wasn't difficult to see why Annie loved it so much. Sure, Texas had its own share of valleys and canyons, but nothing to rival the scenery a few yards from where he slept.

What did old man Horace do when there were no tours to be guided? The man didn't talk much, but Dallas heard he had an Indian wife somewhere that he spent the winters with. Too bad. He might have been able to shed some light on Dallas's predicament.

Light footsteps pattered past his door and the light in the hall outside his room was extinguished. The Rollins women were up late. Knowing Annie might be roaming the house did not help Dallas fall asleep. Nor did the snores coming from Mr. Harris's room next door.

Dallas hung his arm off the side of the bed and scratched Hero's head. Mrs. Rollins had never told him the dog had to stay outside. She'd just look at the animal and smile. Probably because of the silly name Billy had given him.

It was no use. Dallas's brain would not slow down enough for him to sleep. He got dressed and commanded Hero to follow. With one hand on the wall to guide them, he led the way to the parlor. If he couldn't sleep, then Dallas might as well write Ma a letter. As long as the tracks were clear, the train still made its daily run for those wanting to experience northern Arizona in the wintertime.

He hated admitting to his mother that he still hadn't professed his feelings to Annie, but maybe another correspondence between them would help clear things up. He lit a lamp beside the desk and sat down to write out his questions.

By the time he'd finished, his eyes were gritty and strained from the dim lighting. Maybe now he could sleep. He'd penned all his thoughts and questions, and within a couple of weeks Ma would answer in all her wisdom. Maybe Pa would pen a line or two and add his thoughts.

It wasn't only his love for Annie Dallas wondered about, but also whether they should stay in Arizona if she said yes to his proposal. He didn't think his family needed him to help run the ranch, but as their son, he felt he should ask their blessing.

He took the lamp with him and headed back up the stairs to his room.

When he gazed upon Annie across the breakfast table the next morning, he couldn't help but smile. She raised her eyebrows and looked at her mother. Mrs. Rollins grinned and raised her glass in a salute. Dallas narrowed his eyes. What secret did the two women share?

They continued to trade amused looks between them until Dallas wanted to storm from the room. Only an idiot couldn't tell they were finding him the subject of some amusement. Poor Mr. Harris seemed oblivious to everything but his meal. Put food in front of him and no one could expect much participation.

"How does Horace know when to arrive back for the first tour?" Maybe Dallas could distract them.

"He said he'd return after the snow melts and the ground dries." Mrs. Rollins buttered a biscuit. "He has no set date. Once we hired you, the poor dear has wanted only to be with his wife. Other than being an extra hand on the tours, he has no other work to do here. You're quite capable of caring for the livestock without him, aren't you?"

She handed the biscuit to Mr. Harris. "If Annie doesn't take over the boardinghouse, and we aren't able to sell the place, both of you men will be out of jobs. I believe Horace sees the inevitable."

Dallas almost told her not to write him off yet. While he didn't have the funds to purchase the property, whether he stayed or not would depend on Annie.

"Mr. Harris and I have decided to marry in the spring under the big pine across the way. We'd like you and Annie to stand up with us."

Maybe that was the secret between her and her daughter. "I'd be honored." Not to mention he could gaze on Annie during the ceremony. Afterward, he'd approach her about their own nuptials and pray she'd say yes.

He'd been a fool during his time here. Fretting over her choice of attire had wasted a lot of time and hurt Annie's tender feelings. If he hadn't been so judgmental, they might already be married. His mouth dried and he choked on a piece of bacon.

If he'd been a smart man, they might even have had a baby on the way already.

23

Annie stood at her favorite overlook of the canyon and breathed deeply of the crisp air with a hint of spring's mildness. Her contract with the Harvey Company had ended the day before, the same day as her mother's nuptials. Annie had promised her newlywed mother she'd have an answer for her today considering the boardinghouse.

After brushing fallen pine needles from her log seat, she smoothed her skirt and sat. She would miss the canyon in all its pink and coral splendor.

"Morning, Miss Annie." Horace strolled past, leading his mule. "Tours will start up soon. I've come to give my notice."

"You're leaving us?" She shaded her eyes and stared into his grizzled face.

"Yes, ma'am. These old bones aren't what they used to be. I could maybe care for the livestock." He removed his stained leather hat. "But the younger fella can handle that just fine. When I signed on with you last spring, why...I thought I could handle a few months away from my old lady, but she's harping on me something awful." He grinned, revealing teeth stained with tobacco. "She actually misses me when I'm gone."

"I'm happy for you, Horace. Mother should be inside, finishing up her breakfast."

Annie wanted to cry. Here was the opportunity she'd always wanted. Once her mother left with Mr. Harris, Annie could do what she wanted. She could be the second guide with Dallas. But she'd failed miserably on her first camping trip, hadn't liked it as much as she'd thought she would, and the last she'd heard about Dallas's plans were that he was heading back to Texas. She might as well tell her mother to sell the house. Miss Cartwright would be pleased if Annie renewed her contract. She wouldn't be as pleased if Annie requested a transfer, but she couldn't stay by the canyon if everyone else left. Her heart couldn't take it.

Oh, how she would miss being here, remembering the times she'd sat in this exact spot with her father. Mother didn't understand. She'd just say, "Why sit and stare at something you've already seen thousands of times?"

The fact that Annie was turning twenty in a few days and was still unmarried was nobody's fault but her own. She'd had proposals aplenty working at the restaurant, and it wasn't any secret that Sean had had his eye on her as well. But the only man Annie wanted was a tall Texan, and she'd been too foolish to tell him so.

She turned and watched as Dallas strolled up the

walk toward the house, opening an envelope as he went. He'd been having regular correspondence with someone, and she couldn't help but wonder whether he'd found a girl back home to exchange letters with. He'd seemed happier lately, his face lighting up with each letter.

It was none of her business. Annie lifted her face to the midmorning sun and gave her failed hopes and dreams to God. Only He could bring light out of the darkness she felt in her heart. Only He could give her the courage to do what she'd vowed to do two months ago: tell Dallas her true feelings.

Now that he'd returned from his errands, there was no better time. She stood and straightened her skirt, then squared her shoulders and marched toward the house. "Dallas, may I speak with you?"

"Certainly." He grinned. "I was going to hunt you down in a moment."

She eyed the mail in his hand. "An important letter?"

"Very." His eyes twinkled as he propped one booted foot on the top step. "It's from my mother. I've been corresponding with her about a rather...difficult situation."

"Oh?" Annie's palms began to sweat as the look in his eyes intensified. What had she done that warranted his writing to his mother? She fingered the lace at her throat. Maybe she was putting the cart before the horse. He hadn't said anything about the letter being about her.

"Dallas." Horace stepped onto the porch. "Might I have a word with you?"

"Can it wait?" Dallas turned from Annie to the older man.

"Nope. I'm heading out."

Dallas put a hand on Annie's arm. "Don't go anywhere. I'll be right back."

She nodded, took a seat in one of the rockers and caressed the smooth wood of the arm. Soon, someone else would sit in the chairs made by her father. Sleep under the roof he'd built. She gazed down the road. Someone else would attend the simple, clapboard church that was too cold in the winter and often stuffy in the summertime. Tears stung her eyes.

She wasn't foolish enough to think that a woman could run a boardinghouse alone. Mother may have been unmarried, but she'd had Annie's help. Annie could bake as well as she could, and had a more modern way of improving the business, but without someone to help, it would be a lonely job.

Setting the rocker into motion with her foot, she allowed herself to daydream, wondering what it would be like to change the name to the Baker Boardinghouse. It had a nice ring to it, in her opinion. Dallas would be gone soon enough. It wouldn't hurt for Annie to dream.

"Now, what were you wanting to talk to me about?"

She jerked at Dallas's question, suddenly nervous about telling him of her love. "Uh, you first? We were discussing your letter."

"Oh, yes." His mouth quirked. "I suppose Horace told you he was no longer employed here?"

"He mentioned it." Annie cocked her head. What could Horace possibly have to do with her and Dallas? Or the letter in Dallas's hand?

"Would you care to take a walk with me, Annette Rollins?" Dallas's eyes darkened. "What I have to say is very important, and I'd like to have a bit of privacy."

Her mouth dried up, preventing her from answering.

She nodded and let him lead her to the canyon's edge.

*

In the letter that now lay folded in his breast pocket, his mother told Dallas how much of a fool he was for not proposing to Annie before now, and that he was not allowed to return to Texas until he did, and then for only a short time. In simple, straightforward language, Ma advised him to marry the girl and run the boardinghouse.

Now to get Annie to say yes. He wouldn't blame her if she slapped him and marched away. He'd taken much too long getting to this point.

Once he judged they were far enough away from the house not to be overheard, he stopped and faced her. His hands trembled so badly he shoved them in his pockets. What if she said no? He thought she returned his affections. The looks she gave him when she figured he wasn't looking supported that assumption, but even Annie could lose patience with a fool like him.

He took her hands in his. "I've been a fool, putting expectations and restrictions on you that I had no right to do. God made you perfect. You and your split skirts and modern opinions." He swallowed against the mountain in his throat. "Can you forgive me? We've lost so much time because of my prejudice."

"Is that what your letter said? That you were a fool?" Annie's lips twitched.

"Well, my mother did write words like those in the letter." He returned Annie's smile. "Those and a few more choice phrases."

Tears filled her eyes. "I need to tell you something before you say goodbye."

"Wait." He frowned. "I—"

She pulled her hands out of his and laid a finger on his lips. "Please let me finish. I love you, Dallas Baker. From almost the first moment I saw you. No man has infuriated me more, challenged me more and made life worth living more than you have. I want you to know that before you go."

"Why are you just now telling me this?" He gripped her hands again. "Annie, I thought you saw me as nothing more than a friend, .maybe because I took away your dream." His heart danced. She loved him! But wait. Why was she crying? Did she just say goodbye?

"I intend to let my mother sell the house, and I'll renew my contract."

He tightened his hold on her hands. "You haven't renewed your contract yet, have you? If so, you can march right over there and break it." He knelt in front of her, unmindful of the pebbles digging into his knees. "I love you, Annette Rollins. I have from the instance you whirled on me with fire in your eyes. Only I was too stupid to admit it. Then I waited for you to become something you were never meant to be." He hung his head.

"Ma had a few choice words about that, I can tell you." He raised his eyes and locked gazes with her. "I want to marry you. I want you to be my partner guiding folks down into the canyon. We can hire someone to run the boardinghouse. Every day will be like a honeymoon."

"Stand up, please." Her tears escaped, running down her face in streams.

He stood. "Say yes, Annie."

"Are you proposing to me because you want to or because your ma will thrash you if you don't?"

"Because I love you with every fiber of my being. Say yes, Annie. Please." He couldn't bear it if she said no. His heart would shatter into a million pieces, dotting the dark expanse of his soul like the stars in the sky. He would never recover from her rejection.

"I have one condition." She smiled. "I don't want to be a tour guide any longer. I'll stay and run the boardinghouse and leave the adventure to you."

"Does this mean yes?"

She nodded, a grin stretching her face. "Yes."

He put his hands around her waist, lifted her in the air and whooped. When he lowered her back to the ground, he claimed her lips. His world became perfect. "Forgive me?"

She cupped his face. "Definitely. And I'll have a surprise for you on our wedding day."

"I can't wait. Marry me now."

"Silly. I'll need a couple of days." Hooking her arm through his, she pulled. "Let's go tell Mother and Mr. Harris. They'll be pleased and Mother can plan a wedding for the week's end."

"That's five days!" A long time to wait before marrying the girl of his dreams.

"But if you send a telegram, perhaps your mother could attend our wedding." Annie giggled. "After all, she did order you to marry me. Shouldn't she be here to make sure you follow that order?"

"That will set the wedding day back even further, but you're right." He planted a kiss on Annie's forehead. "Ever the thoughtful one. Of course I'd love my family to be here."

"Then we'll set the date for one week from this weekend."

He groaned. "You keep setting it back further and further."

"Maybe you shouldn't have waited so long to tell me you love me." She patted his cheek. "This is your punishment."

"You waited, too." He smiled into her beautiful face. "But you were worth the wait." He pulled her close for another kiss.

24

"Oh, Annie." Mother's eyes flicked over her wedding outfit, her eyes widening. "You look beautiful and…unconventional."

Annie giggled and hugged her. "I think Dallas will be pleasantly surprised."

She turned and lifted her veil from the bed. White rosettes set into a nest of lace and gauze fell to her waist. She set the headband into place and twirled. The motion made her skirt swirl, showing the white boots on her feet. She felt like a princess.

"You are gorgeous." Mrs. Baker stepped into the room, flanked on each side by younger replicas of herself. Annie had met Dallas's sisters the day before and fallen in love with them immediately. "Wait until my boy gets a look at you."

"I'm so glad we waited for your arrival, Mrs. Baker, although I must admit, Dallas was a handful to manage.

God did not give that man a lot of patience." Annie secured her veil with hairpins.

"Please call me Ma Baker. You'll soon be the newest Mrs. Baker." She went to stand next to Annie's mother. "How does it feel to have your baby leave the nest?"

Mother chuckled. "I'm actually the one who's flying the coop, and I'm thrilled. We'll stay until they return from their honeymoon, then we're off to wherever the railroad takes us."

"How exciting." Ma Baker clapped her hands. "All right, Annie. Are you ready?"

"Yes." Her heart fluttered. In mere minutes she would become Dallas's wife. "I'm ready." She took a deep breath and headed down the stairs.

The wedding would take place in her favorite spot beside the canyon. The El Tovar management had donated an organ for the event and the wedding march would begin the moment she stepped onto the porch. Dallas would be able to watch her approach across the lawn.

She may not have known her true heart's desire, but God had, and now her dream waited for her. God had given her a man who loved her for who she was and not for who she might become. Sure, it had taken awhile for Him to open Dallas's eyes, but now Annie knew her future husband loved her without reservation.

Mr. Harris held the front door open while Mother and the others headed outside. Annie stepped out behind them. Her breath caught.

The early evening light dappled the area under the pine trees with a rosy glow. The sun had just begun its descent into the canyon, casting the steep walls in hues of lavender and navy. Sunset was the perfect time to pledge her love to her new husband.

Her legs trembled as she moved down the steps. The organ music sang out at her approach. Dallas turned.

*

Tears blurred his vision, but not before he'd caught sight of his beautiful bride in a white split skirt and button top boots. A gauzy veil obscured her face. He laughed and held out his hand to welcome her. "My beautiful rebel."

Her eyes glistened as she glanced up at him. A smile teased her lips. "I had it made special for today. I'm glad you like it."

"I can't imagine you wearing anything else on our wedding day."

Her hands trembled as he took them in his. His gaze locked with hers through her veil while McMurray officiated. Being the only pastor in town now, he had graciously congratulated Dallas and Annie and agreed to unite them in marriage. Now, he read from his Bible in his slight Irish brogue.

Dallas heard none of it, so engrossed was he in the fact that the beautiful woman in front of him was becoming his wife.

"Mr. Baker?"

Dallas turned to McMurray. "Excuse me?"

The crowd tittered, many of them Annie's friends from the hotel.

"I asked you to repeat after me." McMurray chuckled. "Are you ready, Mr. Baker?"

Dallas nodded and complied. When Annie said, "I do", his tears swelled again. He blinked them away, wanting nothing to detract from his vision of her face.

"You may now kiss your bride."

It wasn't their first kiss, but kissing Annie as her husband was the sweetest thing he'd ever experienced. His heart soared across the canyon as his lips met hers.

Thank you, God, for opening my eyes and giving me such a gift!

He closed his eyes and dipped her over his arm.

~

Don't miss the other Harvey Girl stories:
    Guiding With Love
    Serving With Love
    Warring With Love

ABOUT THE AUTHOR

www.cynthiahickey.com

Cynthia Hickey is a multi-published and best-selling author of cozy mysteries and romantic suspense. She has taught writing at many conferences and small writing retreats. She and her husband run the publishing press, Winged Publications. They live in Arizona and Arkansas, becoming snowbirds with three dogs. They have ten grandchildren who keep them busy and tell everyone they know that "Nana is a writer."

www.ingramcontent.com/pod-product-compliance
Lightning Source LLC
LaVergne TN
LVHW012017060526
838201LV00061B/4350